CARANNA BARO AND THE LEGACY MARK

A FAMILY LEGACY PREQUEL

IULIANA FOOS

G Publishing Partners, LLC

A FAMILY LEGACY SERIES

You can find the series page HERE!

Want updated information on new releases?
Click HERE to sign up for the Newsletter.

Happiness is a rare commodity in the middle of a centuries-long war dividing the galaxy.

Born and raised in times of war, Caranna Baro refuses to settle for being a powerful sorceress. She craves recognition, the Dark Lady title, and she stops at nothing to reach her goal. But she needs a mentor to guide and train her further for the gruesome trials and everyday life ahead.

Tyren Tebbet, is the youngest Dark Lord ever to lead the Defense Circle. He is hated as much as he is feared, not only by the enemy, but by his own people too. When another attempt on his life takes place, an unexpected ally, a young up and coming sorceress, changes his life forever.

Overtaken by their feelings for each other, Caranna and Tyren fight together, keeping one another alive despite the never-ending threat pouring from all directions.

Can they defeat fate and build a life together, or will the mark she carries bring destruction to rain over them, turning their dreams into ashes?

**This is a sweet, closed door romance for ages 14+.

To my friend, Michelle, who not only pushed me forward on the path to becoming an author, but also held my hand through it. Without you, none of my books would've existed.

Thank you, Michelle, for teaching me the things I had no idea I should know. Your guidance and patience are, and will always be close and dear to my heart.

To all my family and friends who believed in me when I didn't, thank you for your support.

Brenda, your honesty, knowledge, and friendship are precious and make me one of the luckiest people in the world to have you on my side.

Tanya, you're the most encouraging person I know. Each of your words pushed me forward to a better version of myself.

One of the scenes in this book has been inspired by an image provided by Amanda Petersen. Thank you so much for the inspiration.

Thank you, to all the ladies in my private group for your kind and encouraging words.

Caranna Baro and the Legacy Mark
A Family Legacy Prequel
COPYRIGHT©2021
IULIANA FOOS
Cover Design by Wren Taylor

Published in the United States of America by:

DLG Publishing Partners

San Antonio, TX 78217

www.DLGPublishingPartners.com

Caranna

My first assignment.

Caranna wiped her sweaty palms over the hips of her brand-new leather outfit. With a deep breath, she opened the door and entered the office she knew all too well.

"How can I help you?" Her professor, one of the few people who ever believed in her, stared at the lit-up screens on his desk.

"Lord Garnik," she bowed her head with respect, "I am here in response to your message, to receive my first assignment." Caranna placed her travel bag by the door.

Confusion covered his sharp features for a moment. One of the best sorcerers she knew, the older man before her had been the one who had trained her since she'd been a child. Overhead lights danced in his silvery hair, reminding her that she'd first met him about twelve years ago.

"If I didn't recognize your voice and your unique energy signature, I would've thought you were an impostor." Professor Garnik rose and walked around his desk. "Look at you." He measured her from head to toe. "Now your appearance matches that fierce sorceress inside you."

The intensity of his stare made Caranna self-conscious, and she tugged at the edges of the long, sleeveless duster.

A slight twitch of amusement tugged at the corner of her lips. Her maid, Fira, hardly recognized her a couple of weeks ago when she'd gotten her makeover. Cutting her long, curly, silver hair to a shoulder length, and permanently changing the color to jet black, had completely transformed her look.

"Like you said so many times, professor, people need to take me seriously."

"They sure will now." The older man nodded, then returned to his desk. "Are you ready for your first assignment?"

"Yes, I have my travel bag ready." Caranna pointed her thumb over a shoulder.

"Good, I noticed you've added your name to the list of knights looking for a mentor to prepare you for the Lordship trials." Her professor sat, gesturing to the chair across his desk.

"Yes, I did." Caranna sat on the edge of the seat, her shoulders stiff.

"I don't want you to get your hopes up. Do you know how very few of the Dark Lords take women as apprentices?" He lifted his gaze to her. "Not to mention, there are very few without an apprentice at the moment."

"I know it's a long shot." She let out a sigh. "But I have graduated first in my class." Pride filled her heart.

"And for a good reason." Lord Garnik nodded again. "You are powerful, and disciplined. With a little luck, you may become one of our best sorcerers." A smile parted his thin lips. "Even better than me."

"Thank you, professor." Embarrassment burned the tips of her ears.

"I pulled a few strings and got you an assignment on the world of Brillum." He interlaced his fingers and leaned back in his chair. "It might not be the easiest one, but it is an opportunity for you."

"Brillum is the place where we are mining the Brill crystals for the cloaking devices, correct?" Caranna quickly found the reference in her mind.

"Yes, and it's also where Dark Lord Tyren Tebbet is stationed at the moment. He has asked for enforcements."

A chill coursed her back at the sound of the dark lord's name. His reputation preceded him, one of the most feared, difficult to work with, and merciless lords in the Federation—the youngest leader ever of the Defense Circle.

"And you're sending me?" Caranna stood, already wary to face the man who she'd only encountered once before.

"Don't underestimate yourself." Her professor leaned forward. "You are the best up and coming sorceress in our ranks."

Caranna shook her head. "He won't be happy to see me." Memories from almost six years ago filled her mind.

The Dark Lord Tebbet had visited the training grounds at the academy once, and she—only fifteen back then—struggled with her sword skills. She still did, but at least now, she'd mastered her energy attacks—deadlier than any weapon.

At the time, he stopped in front of her. Tall and broad, she didn't even reach to his shoulder. Disgust reflected in his golden eyes when he looked down at her as if she was an insect.

'You are better off becoming an exotic dancer than a knight. You have no business being here.' His words, still vivid in her mind, stung her.

"Change his mind. Let him see who you have become." Professor Garnik stood. "You have been assigned a ship. It's waiting for you in hangar number eighty-four, fully stocked and fueled, ready to take off."

Caranna inhaled a gulp of air. "Thank you, professor."

"You also have two droids on board. One household model, and a pilot assist one." For a second time, the man who had taught her so much walked around his desk.

Caranna's hope to make a name for herself, climb the ranks ladder, and claim a respectable position within the order, shook from its foundation.

"Lord Tebbet only had two apprentices in the past." Professor Garnik lowered his voice. "Both of them turned against him, and he was forced to kill them. You know it's not uncommon for this to happen."

"Yes." Caranna nodded. "And it's also a frequent occurrence to have mentors turning against their apprentices when they become powerful enough to present a threat."

"True." He sighed. "But Lord Tebbet is not one of them. He lives with honor. Some say he's a little too rigid, but personally, I am an admirer of his morals." The older professor walked her near the door. "Try to see beyond the rumors. He has many enemies, most jealous and afraid of him. Just be yourself, and you'll be fine."

He gave her wrist a small, encouraging squeeze, as he used to do before her tests.

"I have to admit, I'm not looking forward to this assignment. I was hoping for something else." Caranna squared her shoulders. She was no longer the little girl from a few years ago, and she'd learned a thing or two.

"Trust me, it's the best opportunity for you."

"But professor, he's not even a sorcerer. Lord Tebbet is a guardian." She grasped onto the first excuse passing through her mind. "Perhaps you could assign me to someone else?"

Lord Garnik shook his head. "A sorcerer

wouldn't have much to teach you. Someone from a completely different class than yours is who you want as mentor."

With a sigh, Caranna picking up her travel bag from the floor, then opened the door and stepped outside the office.

"Thank you for everything, professor."

"May the energies serve your will." He smiled, then took a step forward. "And pick up a sword on your way out. It can't hurt." The door closed before she had the chance to say anything else.

Bag over a shoulder, Caranna walked to the hangar, excited to finally have her own ship. She didn't need to buy a sword, she had one. Her father's sword hilt lay in the bottom of her bag, the only thing she had left of him. She had never met him, but her great grandmother always said he had died a hero.

Here we go. My first assignment might not bring me much, but it's a start. Head held high, she marched through the opened, double doors of the spaceport.

2

Tyren

EYES CLOSED and fingers pinching the bridge of his nose, Tyren leaned back in his chair. For hours he'd been reading through reports following the movements of the Coalition's troops.

The world of Brillum was an independent, shared planet, by both federation and coalition forces. Mining the Brill crystals, crucial in cloaking technology, had always been a priority.

With both factions on the same planet, his job involved more routine than he would've liked. Keeping an eye on the enemy's movements was boring at best.

He glanced toward the screen displaying the time.

Time for my evening round. Tyren stood, stretching.

His bracer rang, and he checked the name. *Not again.*

Shoulders slumped, he let himself fall back in the chair, transferring the incoming videocall to the larger screen on his desk.

"Yes, Mother." Tyren connected the call despite his first instinct, to ignore it. He wouldn't have heard the end of it if he had.

"Tyren, are you coming home this weekend?" His mother's sharp, noble features filled the screen.

"Are you forgetting where I am?" He settled in for another fight with her. "I can't just drop everything and come for a visit."

"There is this girl I would like you to meet." His mother waved a dismissive hand. "She's from a good family, and willing to meet you."

Willing to meet me? What am I, a pariah?

Tyren shook his head. "I've told you a hundred times, Mother. The answer is still no. Please stop trying to force all those doll-girls on me."

"Well, I am not getting any younger here, and it would be nice to have a grandchild while I'm still alive." Her face scrunched with the same expression she used every time she tried to make him feel guilty. "You are getting older, and the pool of women willing to even consider you, smaller."

"I just turned thirty." Tyren stood. "How's that old?"

"You need to get married, settle down, and have some babies." His mother squared her shoulders, the authoritarian tone in her voice perfectly matching her posture.

"I will get married when I meet the woman who captures my heart." Tyren made an effort to remain calm, returning to his seat. "Not to mention that I like a woman with a little more personality than a doorknob. Those *noble* girls of yours are not even close."

"How many times do I have to tell you that marriage and love have nothing to do with one another?"

The snappy undertone in his mother's voice scaled up.

Memories from a distant childhood invaded his mind. His parents had never loved each other. Even if he was only a child back then, he'd always sensed the resentment between the two of them. An energy user, his father was rarely home.

I can't even blame him. Who would want to go to a loveless home?

But his parent's relationship had taught him one thing—it was not what he wanted for himself.

"Right. I saw how that that worked for you and Father." Tyren stood again, anger pushing him to his feet. "I'll let fate decide for me."

"I just hope you won't bring home some commoner." His mother lifted her head with pride, and disgust coated the word *commoner*.

"I will bring home the woman who will have my heart. I don't care about nobility, and you know it." Fists closed, Tyren stood his ground. It wasn't the first time they had the exact same discussion.

His mother let out a sigh. "All my friends have grandkids, showing them off at all our gatherings." She wiped a nonexistent tear from the corner of her eye. "I have nothing to show."

Boiling fury forced Tyren to take a deep breath. "Then borrow a baby if that's the latest fashion trend among your friends."

His mother's attitude changed, as if he'd hit a switch. A perfect smile parted her lips.

"Tyren, I know that your job is important. Without you and the troops you're commanding, we would have those awful coalition barbarians stomping all over the place, but you have to start thinking about yourself, too."

"This is my life, Mother. Being an energy user is not a job." Tyren cut the air in front of him with an open palm.

Every time he had an argument with his mother, he missed his father. Growing up, training, he'd connected with his father away from home. His father hadn't climbed the ranks ladder, choosing to stop at being a Dark Lord, and teaching the young students at the Academy. But he taught him everything he knew, including the wisdom of a simple man.

"You've already reached the top. Maybe you should start considering retirement. Do what all the nobles do." His mother didn't appear to be done making her point. "The position you have with the Dark Circle is the highest anyone can dream of. You've had it for the past six years, and it's a known fact that nobody stays there much longer. Those people of yours will try to kill you."

Fear reflected in his mother's eyes.

"Many have already tried and failed. Trust me, I'm here to stay." Tyren squared his shoulders.

"You need to do what's expected from you as a member of this family, a highly respected noble. All decent men run their family business, look after the safety and well-being of their families."

"Without us, the energy users who protect all of you, none of them would have the chance to do that. Not to mention that I've been running the family business for the past eight years, since Father died." Tyren glanced toward the screen to his left.

A short message confirmed the troops he'd asked for were on their way, with an estimated arrival time for the next morning.

Finally, some good news. Now if only I could get some support from the energy users, we'd be in great shape here.

"Am I boring you?" His mother's voice yanked him back to their argument.

"It is time for me to make my rounds, Mother." Tyren grabbed his gloves. "And for the last time, please stay out of my bedroom. I will live my life the way I see fit."

"You're just like your father." A defeated undertone made her voice drop with resignation. "Your exaggerated sense of duty will destroy you." Without another word, she disconnected the call.

"That's the nicest thing you ever said to me, Mother." Tyren muttered under his breath and pulled his gloves on. "I only wish Father would've lived long enough to see me becoming what he always thought I would." He hit the button on his desk turning off the communication system, then started to the door.

After a couple of steps, he stopped and glanced back to the black screen. His mother wasn't entirely wrong. Lately, he caught himself wishing for someone to share his accomplishments and failures with.

But women from his mother's world would never understand his morals, his sense of duty to his people.

Perhaps an energy user? A sorceress? His mind ventured into a fantasy world, where that one perfect woman would cross paths with him.

He wanted the experience of falling in love, feeling like he couldn't breathe away from the woman he loved. He'd seen others living that dream, he'd sensed their emotions, and couldn't stop thinking he would never have that luxury.

Tyren took a deep breath. He didn't mind carrying the burden and responsibility that came with his position, but at times, loneliness circled around his heart, like a dark, hungry beast.

Maybe one day. He shook his head and exited his office.

3

Caranna

BRIGHT GOLDEN-HUED SKIES welcomed Caranna when she landed her ship on Brillum.

"AI, you're in charge of the ship." She activated her breather and sealed the door leading to the exit chamber.

During her ten-hour flight from Forrison, she'd rested long enough to face a new day, and researched all the information she could find about the world of Brillum. With a different air composition, humans needed to wear masks outside.

The acclimatization cycle ended with a whistle, and the hatch slid open. A wave of strong energy flew through her, as if someone had turned up a dial. Brillum's uncommonly high alignment with the energies took her breath away.

Micro crystals fell from the golden sky like glittering snow. One hand stretched forward, she caught some on the palm of her hand. Cold to the touch, they felt like snow, but the microcrystals didn't melt on contact with her skin.

If it wasn't for the inconvenience of the unbreathable air, this would be a beautiful world.

A smile stretched her lips, and Caranna started toward the main building.

Soldiers and workers roamed the area, and oversized lifters loaded cargo ships with precious Brill minerals, to be transported to the processing plants.

Under the bright sky, everything around seemed dipped in gold, the light reflecting in subtle tones. She glanced at her exposed shoulder, and even her own skin seemed to have changed color to a soft golden glow.

In the distance, green, fuchsia, and orange clouds mixed in a variety of breathtaking colors. *Pretty.*

The surreal reality of the scene reclaimed its spot in her mind, overriding the surrounding beauty of nature. She was about to report for duty, and she didn't look forward to facing Dark Lord Tyren Tebbet.

"Excuse me." Inside the building, she stopped the first officer in sight.

"Yes?" The man faced her with a bright blue gaze, measuring her from head to toe. "How can I help you?" A more than polite smile parted his lips.

"Could you please tell me where Lord Tebbet's office is?" Caranna deactivated the translucent shield covering her face.

"Of course. I was on my way to my office, a few doors away from Lord Tebbet's." He gestured to an elevator a few steps ahead. "I'll walk you there."

"Thank you." She avoided a group of soldiers headed toward the exit.

"I'm Major Marek. Darion Marek." He clicked his heels and bowed his head. "I assume you're a sorceress?" The major pressed a button on the wall panel marked with a downward arrow.

"Yes, I am. Caranna Baro." She tilted her head and squared her shoulders with pride. "Class three sorceress."

The man's eyes rounded with a mix of surprise and admiration. "As far as I know, a class three is pretty high. You must be powerful."

After years spent trying to prove herself, Caranna's heart filled with joy at the sight of his reaction. Non energy users in the federation had always respected her kind.

"Not as high as first class, but not bad." She gazed at the screen showing the elevator in motion.

The door slid open and Major Marek invited her in, then followed her inside.

"The offices are on the lowest level." He pressed the bottom button of the four, and the thick metal doors closed.

"Good to know." She doubted she'd spend a long time on Brillum, but determination pushed Caranna forward. She would do whatever it took to impress Dark Lord Tebbet.

"You must be new here. I would remember if I'd seen you before." His insistent gaze swept over her frame again.

"Yes, I'm reporting for duty." Caranna tugged at the edges of her leather duster.

"Maybe I could show you around after you're done with Lord Tebbet?" Another wide smile parted his lips.

Should she tell him that Lord Tebbet might reject her and send her off world, or give the guy false hope?

He seems genuinely interested.

"I'm not sure how this first meeting will work out." Caranna opted for the truth. "I'll have to let you know."

"Fair enough." Major Marek nodded, then glanced toward the panel display. The last of the four squares lit up and the doors swished open.

A long corridor with numerous doors welcomed Caranna from the first step outside the elevator.

"Lord Tebbet's office is the one at the end," the major pointed to the right side, "the one with the guards."

Of course, it is. She resisted rolling her eyes.

Caranna counted four soldiers in shiny armor, two on each side of an opening. "Thank you."

I have to make this work. I need to. She gathered courage and determination from years of being overlooked, pushed to the side, and left last on anyone's choice.

"This is my stop." Major Marek halted in front of a door—his name printed in black letters on a silver plaque. "Hopefully, everything goes all right and we'll see each other again."

"Maybe." Caranna forced a smile and continued her way forward. "Thank you again for your help." She glanced back over a shoulder.

"My pleasure." The major smiled and entered his office.

Each step closer to Lord Tebbet's office sent the ever-annoying ants of doubt through her veins.

Unlike the other offices, the absence of a door revealed an antechamber, with one man seated at a desk. Two of the guards drew closer stopping her.

"I'm reporting for duty." Chin held high, she tried to project the confidence she lacked inside.

"Let her through." The man behind the desk stood. "You must be the new sorceress, Caranna Baro?" He met her halfway with a short nod and stiff shoulders. "I'm lieutenant Sargon."

"Yes, I am. A pleasure meeting you, Lieutenant. I'm here to see Lord Tebbet." Caranna held her breath.

"Unfortunately, he's not here. More troops arrived this morning, and he is inspecting them." The lieutenant gestured to the only chair placed in front of his desk. "If you'd like to, you may wait here."

"I prefer not to waste any time." Caranna let out a breath, relaxing. "If you could tell me where exactly I can find Lord Tebbet, I'll be on my way." She took a couple of steps closer to the guards.

"As soon as you exit the building, go right. You

can't miss the thousand new soldiers lined in formation." Lieutenant Sargon returned to his desk but remained standing.

"Thank you." She faced the doorway, took another few steps toward the exit, then glancing back over a shoulder she reconfirmed with the lieutenant. "Out the building and to the right. Got it."

One more step and she thudded into something hard. Quickly turning her head in the direction she walked, she faced a wide, armored chest. Scars marked two thick arms, and Caranna lifted her gaze, ready to yell at the guard blocking her way.

A pair of gold eyes looked down at her with a mix of annoyance and curiosity.

"You should look ahead, in the direction you're walking, not behind." The deep, raspy voice that once told her she had no business being in the Academy of Dark Arts, hit her with the same recognition as the gold eyes.

"Lord Tebbet." The involuntary whisper left her lips, and she took a step back.

I couldn't have made a worse impression if I had tried.

He nodded. "And who are you?"

Caranna gathered all the shards of her shattered dignity. "Sorceress Caranna Baro reporting for duty, My Lord." She bowed her head with respect.

The thick, scar-laced arms crossed over his chest, and a deep crease appeared between his brows. "What kind of duty?"

"Professor Garnik sent me here." She looked up, trying to see what kind of impression she'd made. "I'm the enforcement you have requested."

She still barely reached his shoulder, and his intimidating stature was only topped by the forced laughter now coming from his lips.

"Good professor Garnik is losing his mind in old age." Lord Tebbet walked by her. "I asked for an enforcement, not a fledgling in need of babysitting."

"I am a third-class sorcerer." Anger boiled under her skin, causing her fists to close by her sides.

It wasn't the first time he'd insulted her, it hurt just as before and angered her twice as much.

Lord Tebbet opened the door on the right side of the antechamber, stopped, then faced her with a laser sharp gaze.

"You're lying. You are too young to be a third-class sorcerer."

"I am not. You may check my file in the Academy's Archive." She took a step forward, each muscle in her body tensed. "I graduated two weeks ago, first in my class."

"Go home, girl." Lord Tebbet waved a dismissive hand, turning his back to her.

The hell I will. You have humiliated me twice, now.

Anger slipped from under her control, and golden lightning shot from Caranna's fingertips, landing around the man who dismissed her before giving her a chance.

"What in the stars do you think you're doing attacking me?" Hand closed on his sword, Lord Tebbet walked toward her.

The threat in each of his steps didn't scare her, but they did ring all the alarms in her head. Behind her, the guards closed in until he signaled them to stand back.

A thick, terrifying blade poured from the hilt of his weapon.

"If I wanted to attack you, you'd be dead." Caranna took a step back. "I only wanted to get your attention."

Without any hesitance, his sword lifted above her head.

Bright gold ribbons of light shot from her left

hand, closing around his wrist, and stopping the descent of the blade coated in crimson lighting.

"You've got my attention, now." He growled the words between clenched jaws. "Not something you should have wished for."

Caranna focused, maintaining the energy shackle around his arm. But Lord Tebbet was more powerful than she'd anticipated, and the effort of holding him from striking her, made her hand shake.

"I'm not a little girl for you to dismiss." She tried to hide the real effect his power had on her. Countering his sheer physical strength drained her stored energy.

Sometimes I wish I could just punch someone in their face. Or kick them where it hurts.

A piercing and inquiring gaze stared at her. "Your eyes. I've seen them before." He drew closer. "Have we met?"

"Once, six years ago." Caranna channeled her inner anger, finding the strength to stand against him. "Just like now, you insulted me back then too."

His left arm moved suddenly, shooting a ball of blood-red energy toward her.

Quick in reaction, she countered the blow with a golden one, causing a powerful explosion.

She flew backward, her back slammed against the wall on the left side of the antechamber. Opposite to her, Lord Tebbet had been pushed into his office.

Caranna collected herself from the floor. Beside her, the guards scrambled to rise to their feet, closing around her.

From his office, Lord Tebbet appeared in the doorway. "Come in. We need to talk."

The guards looked at each other, hesitant, but let her pass.

At least I made my point.

Head held high, she entered his office, closing the door behind her.

"Six years ago." Lord Tebbet gestured to one of the two chairs facing each other in front of his desk. "You used to have long, silver hair." He appeared to remember exactly the moment haunting her ever since.

"That's right." She nodded, refusing to sit.

"I see you proved me wrong. You have become a powerful sorceress against my suggestion to try your luck with a dancing career." Lord Tebbet clasped his hands behind him. "And for the record, you're above a class three."

Satisfaction filled her heart, a smile tugged at the

corners of her mouth. "It's the highest that can be awarded at graduation."

"Why are you here?" He paced the width of his office.

"Professor Garnik gave me this assignment yesterday." She straightened her spine, a thin layer of cold sweat covering her palms.

"Why you? Why here? Why now?" Lord Tebbet stopped in front of her.

The intensity of his gaze cut through her, deeper than any blade ever could. For a moment, she felt vulnerable, exposed.

"This is my first assignment—"

"Not what I asked you." A foot taller than her, he bent over to her level. "The real reason. What exactly do you want? Nobody volunteers to work with me without an agenda. What's yours?"

Throat dry, Caranna swallowed a gulp of air. Her professor's advice, to be herself, flashed in her mind. For a split moment, she was tempted to lie, but opted for the truth.

"Professor Garnik thought you would be the perfect mentor for me." She held his gaze.

"Do you think so too?" Unblinking, he stared at her, as if he tried to read her thoughts.

"I'm not sure. But I do know that I need a mentor to prepare for next year's lordship trials."

Hesitation, tension, and something between curiosity and suspicion, held the feared dark lord in place, only a couple of inches from her face.

"Garnik should know better. I'm not looking for an apprentice." Lord Tebbet walked away from her, sitting at his desk. "I have already killed two."

"I know." Caranna clasped her hands together in front of her. "But I'm not like them."

Lord Tebbet measured her from the top of her head to the tips of her boots, a deep crease marking his forehead.

"I will talk to professor Garnik. You will have my answer before the end of the day." He powered up a couple of screens on his desk, focusing his attention on the luminous panels. "Feel free to visit the base."

4

Tyren

AN AMUSED SMILE tugged at the corner of his lips, and Tyren leaned back in his chair.

Well, damn. I didn't think today would be the day I got an apprentice. He glanced toward the closed door. *I have never seen those guards so confused. For a moment, they didn't know if they should arrest her, or run for their lives.*

The earlier confrontation with the powerful sorceress replayed in his mind, more and more details coming to light. Her delicate features contrasted with the power concealed inside her. But what surprised him most was her honesty, how she admitted her goal without even trying to beat around the subject.

Do I want all the complications that come with an apprentice? What if I'm forced to kill her, too?

Tyren shook his head and inhaled a large gulp of air. Yes, he could use someone to watch his back, but he wasn't sure she wouldn't betray him. From experience, he'd learned that everyone did sooner or later.

He glanced one more time at the door, then dialed a frequency and opened one of the large screens.

Let's see what the good, old professor has to say.

"My Lord." Professor Garnik's voice filled the room before his image appeared on the floating panel.

"Professor. What were you thinking, sending me this girl?" Tyren clasped his hands on the edge of the black desk.

"I was expecting your call." The older man smiled. "Permission to speak freely?"

"Please do. You already know that you don't have to ask." Tyren nodded. "You've been my father's best friend, a second father to me."

"I promised him I'd always watch over you." A shadow passed through the eyes of the old professor. "And by sending Caranna to you, I did just that."

"She's a child." Tyren grasped the first excuse in his mind.

"Not anymore." Lord Garnik's wholehearted laughter made more crinkles appear around his eyes. "She graduated the Academy first in her class, and she's the most powerful up and coming sorceress of this generation."

"She is powerful, indeed." Tyren accepted the one truth he agreed on. "Way above class three."

"You know the rules won't allow us to grade her any higher at the time of graduation. But you are correct, she's close to first class, and she's only twenty-one years old."

"Why her? Why now? Why here?" Tyren tensed.

Was something else involved, something he didn't know about? Yes, he trusted the professor, but what was the young sorceress' role? He tried to quiet the multitude of questions busying his mind.

"I got wind of another plot against you." A loud sigh left the other man's lips. "Tyren, you've made many enemies, and you need someone close to you, to watch your back."

"And this girl is that person?" Doubt coated his words.

She didn't even look where she was walking,

never mind watching my back. He recalled the
moment they met when she walked into him.

"Caranna and you have a lot more in common
than you think. She's not only honest to a fault, but
also uncommonly loyal." The professor drew closer
to the screen. "As your apprentice, she won't raise
any suspicions."

Tyren shook his head. "I've learned to be
prepared any day, any moment for an attack. I don't
need her." He stood, still debating with himself on if
he should accept help or not. "I appreciate you
trying, but I can take care of myself."

"Tyren, there will be an attack soon. This time,
you'll face a small army, and from what I've heard,
they're adding to their numbers." The professor's
voice dropped to a whisper. "You need her. And she
needs you."

"She's a sorceress." In contrast with Lord
Garnik's low voice, Tyren's scaled up. "What can I
teach her?"

"Everything you know. She still can't hold a
sword properly." Professor Garnik leaned back,
distancing himself from the screen. "And to be
honest, she might teach you a thing or two, as well."

"Like what?" Brows furrowed, Tyren tried to
figure out what someone so young could teach him.

"Perhaps, to control that temper of yours that you're so famous for." A grin parted the older man's lips.

Tyren inhaled, then returned to his chair. "From our earlier encounter, it didn't look like she's in control of her emotions. I made her angry and she attacked me."

"Trust me, she didn't. If she wanted to attack you, you would be injured right now. I told her to let you see what she's made of, her power, and to not accept your rejection." Professor Garnik laughed and crossed his arms over his chest. "I assume you dismissed her as soon as she opened her mouth?"

"I did." Tyren had to admit, the old man knew him better than anyone else. "But I still don't think I need her."

"I know your pride won't let you admit it, but I hope you will at least think about it."

"Where are the energy users I asked for?" Tyren preferred to change the subject, and not refuse the professor's offering again. "I need someone to take over this operation, so I can go do other things."

"On their way. The three energy users I sent should arrive tomorrow at the latest." Professor Garnik nodded. "Caranna registered for the next year's lordship trials. You don't have much time to prepare her."

His father's friend's insistence wore heavy on him, and Tyren let out a loud sigh. "I'll think about it. But I can't make any promises. Yet." He stood again, unable to relax.

It wasn't just the news that another attack against him was on the way, but the presence of the young sorceress threw him off his routine.

"Don't take too long."

"I told you a couple of years ago that I wouldn't take apprentices anymore." Tyren straightened his spine, hoping to show determination. "You should call this girl back and give her another assignment."

"This is the best assignment for her." The professor stood in front of the camera. "And for you. I hope you'll realize it before it's too late."

"We'll keep in touch." Tyren lifted a hand to the red button, waiting to terminate the connection.

"We sure will." The other man bowed his head slightly. "May the energies serve your will and show you the right path."

Beating him to it, the professor ended the call first.

The right path. Tyren mused, his eyes still fixed on the blank screen.

If he were to be honest with himself, he liked Caranna. She knew what she wanted and didn't apologize for it. Her power was impressive, and he had to admit, her delicate beauty caught him off guard.

The probability of her turning on him, persisted in his mind, and killing her wasn't on the top of his list.

I like her too much to just end her. What if the professor is wrong and she eventually tries to eliminate me?

Tyren pinched the bridge of his nose and straightened his spine. A loud growl reminded him he hadn't eaten breakfast yet, he'd been too eager to inspect the troops first.

Well, I see how today is playing off. Seems I might get an apprentice, or not. He ran a hand through his hair. *But I would sure like to know her better.*

Out of nowhere, laughter exploded inside him, overflowing in his quiet office.

I'm tempted to take her as my apprentice just to see the look on my mother's face when she sees us together.

5

Caranna

HALF AN HOUR after her encounter with Lord Tebbet, Caranna sat in the cantina at one of the tables by the large window. She closed her hands around a steaming cup of tea.

What do I want? Lord Tebbet to stick to his decision and send me packing, or Professor Garnik to change his mind?

She popped a slice of fruit in her mouth. The tangy-sweet taste exploded on her tongue, and she searched the assortment in the bowl for another piece.

A part of her wanted nothing more than to be

rejected again. She was used to it. For years, rejection had been the force driving her forward. Being Lord Tebbet's apprentice didn't appeal to her. Yet, there was a part that wondered how things would be if just this once, she'd be accepted by someone. By anyone.

But the legendary dark lord, despite his young age, wasn't just anyone. Being his apprentice, alone, would've brought her a reputation.

"Is everything set?" A voice rose from behind her.

Caranna sipped from her lavender tea, hoping for the calming effect it always had on her.

"Yes. The mighty dark lord will get the call in about an hour or so." Another voice answered with a satisfied undertone. "Today is going to be his last."

The mighty dark lord? Are these people talking about Lord Tebbet?

Caranna leaned against the backrest of her chair, focusing her attention on the conversation behind her.

"Hey, did you guys hear about the chick that attacked him in his office today?" A third man chuckled. "Too bad she didn't take him out. We could've just packed and gone home."

"You idiot." The sound of a slap reached Caranna's ears. "If she did, we wouldn't have gotten paid."

They are planning to kill him. The reality hit her like a cold shower.

"True." A deeper voice, belonging to a fourth man, agreed. "But man, I wish I could've seen it. Apparently, she's some young sorceress, fresh out of the Academy. Gutsy."

News travel fast. But how do they know all the details? Is there someone leaking information?

Caranna kept busy munching on another piece of fruit, tensing her hearing to not miss a word.

"Everyone in their positions?" The first one who spoke earlier, seemed to be more focused on the job. "And did you take care of that technician? The one who *won't* be able to fix the problem with the shipping-carts system blocking the mine?"

"Done and done." A proud voice answered him, followed by a forced laugh. "For two thousand credits, he won't find what's wrong, and he will disappear the moment our target comes to the location."

"Perfect. I took care of the guards." The man who had earlier wished he'd seen her in action volunteered his bit of information.

Should I warn him? Will the proof of loyalty tip the balance in my favor? Questions started to form in her mind, like tiny pieces of a puzzle coming together. *Do I want the balance to tilt that way?*

"Good. The rest of the crew are on their way to the mine, gathering in the positions we've discussed." A chair grated on the concrete floor, as if someone pushed it back to stand.

"Are you sure we have enough fire power? Should we try and hire more?" One more chair, followed by another two scraped against the floor.

"There are twenty of us." The deeper voice sounded like he'd started to walk away. "If we can't take him out, damn, the man deserves to live."

The collective laughter moved farther and farther from her, and Caranna finally glanced over a shoulder to see the group walking toward the exit.

Hm. Three bounty hunters and that fourth one looks like a soldier. Quickly, she refocused on her tea. *What do I do?*

Torn between warning Lord Tebbet about the imminent attack, and letting events play out as they would, Caranna hunched over the table, massaging her temples.

Pros and cons danced in her mind, like partners who loved and hated each other at the same time.

Yes, telling him could score her points, and get herself a mentor, but did she want him? There was also a possibility he would suspect her of doing it only to earn his trust and hiding her true intent—of turning against him one day.

Could she live with herself if he got killed, knowing she could've saved his life, and didn't?

I owe it to my peace of mind. I have to tell him, and it's up to him what he does with the information.

As if springs replaced her joints, Caranna stood and ran toward the exit, activating her breather. She scanned the area, hoping to see him, and not wasting time by going to his office again. If he was even still there.

Instead of Dark Lord Tebbet, her gaze stopped on Major Marek, turning around a corner.

"Major." She hurried to him. "Have you by any chance seen Lord Tebbet?

"He's having breakfast." The major pointed behind him, a touch of confusion clouding his blue eyes.

"I'm coming from the cantina. He's not in there." Caranna shook her head.

"The officers and all energy users have a separate lounge. Didn't anyone tell you?" He gestured to the corner of the building.

"No. I'm not on the job yet." She lowered her head for a moment.

Maybe I shouldn't bother him? The hell with his breakfast.

"Where is this lounge?" She stared at the man before her.

"I'll take you in." A smile parted his lips. "You can't get in without a special badge." He tapped over an ID card hanging around his neck.

"Thank you. I appreciate it." Caranna followed him around the same corner he'd turned from only seconds ago.

"I've heard about the meeting." Major Marek chuckled. "Your attack is the talk of the camp."

"It wasn't an attack." Caranna rolled her eyes. She was growing tired of explaining her actions. "I only wanted to make a point."

"You sure did." The major scanned his badge in front of a reader, opening the door. "There he is." He pointed to a table in the back corner of the spacious room.

Unlike the cantina she'd been in, the lounge looked a lot more luxurious, with dark carpet on the floor, black tablecloths, and servers running around instead of a self-serve line and plain metal tables and chairs.

"Thank you again." Caranna deactivated her

breather, stepping through the second set of sliding doors, and beelining toward Lord Tebbet.

"Always a pleasure." The major's words followed her inside.

She smiled at him over a shoulder, without stopping. Time was running short and the fear of being too late pushed her forward, heart accelerating in her chest.

"My Lord." She stopped in front of Lord Tebbet's table, almost out of breath.

"How did you get in here?" He stared at her with the same golden eyes, this time reflecting surprise.

"I had help. May I?" She gestured to the empty chair across from his.

"No. I would like to have my breakfast in peace." He refocused on his food.

"My Lord, permission to speak freely? It's important." Her pulse accelerated with simmering fury. He could've at least remembered his manners.

"If I say no, will you go away?" Defiance weaved around him, like a basket around a hollow center.

Caranna refused to admit herself defeated and sat on the chair across from him, leaning forward.

"I've overheard a conversation between some bounty hunters." She lowered her voice. "There will be an attempt on your life."

"That's Thursday for me." Lord Tebbet impaled a piece of meat. "Nothing new."

"You don't understand." Caranna shook her head. "It's going to be an ambush in the mine—some fake malfunctioning machinery alarm."

"You just happened to hear all this, and volunteered the information?" Suspicion filled his narrowed eyes. "Why?"

"Because it is the right thing to do." Caranna pushed back from the table.

"And it has nothing to do with serving your agenda?" Lord Tebbet lifted a forkful of scrambled eggs to his mouth.

She grabbed his wrist half-way, causing the food to fall back on the plate. "I'm not doing this to get in your graces. I honestly don't care who my mentor will be as long as I get the training I need. You don't like or trust me, and that's mutual." Caranna held his penetrating gaze, releasing his wrist. "I only came here out of respect for Professor Garnik."

"Then maybe you should leave." The dark lord reloaded his fork.

"Maybe, but I am not like the others. If I can save a life, I will." Arms crossed over her chest, Caranna leaned against her chair, and crossed her legs. "I'm not a mindless, power-thirsty—"

"You do seek power." Lord Tebbet swallowed his food and reached for the cup of coffee in front of him. "It is why you want to pass your lordship trials, to climb through the ranks."

"You don't get it, do you?" Caranna tilted her head to the side. "I have no interest in killing you, or anyone else. I need my mentor alive and well, so I can learn everything I need to know, train in areas where I lack. Turning against my mentor would be counterproductive."

With a cold calm, he placed his cup back on the table, then leaned forward. "Do you know what the difference between us is?"

"Other than the obvious?" Caranna arched a brow, half amused by his question.

"I have already climbed the mountain you are going up now. You keep your eyes on the prize and keep moving forward, look for ways to get to the top." He clasped his hands, a couple of scars stretching over his knuckles.

"What's wrong with wanting recognition? I already proved to you that a career as an exotic dancer was not my future." Caranna tensed, uncrossed her legs, and propped her elbows on the edge of the table. "It would be nice to earn the respect I deserve and worked hard for."

"Nothing wrong with that." He slowly moved his head from right to left, only to look at her with more intensity than ever. "But once you reach that top, you learn to look back to the ones who want to pull you down and take your spot."

"I'm not interested in taking your place, or anyone else's. I'd rather share that position with someone I trust and watch each other's backs." Shoulders relaxed, she pushed away from the table for a second time.

The feeling of losing terrain coiled around her, cold and suffocating.

Maybe it's for the best to move on. He really hates me.

"Go home. I will let professor Garnik know that you're on your way." Lord Tebbet's rejection hit her harder than she thought it would.

Her eyes stung, and she fought back tears. The last thing she wanted was to give him any satisfaction. With all the dignity she could muster, Caranna stood.

"Is this your official decision?" Shoulders squared, she suppressed the humiliation for a second time.

"Yes, I don't want you here." Lord Tebbet patted the corner of his mouth with the black napkin.

"When the time comes, I don't want to be the one to kill you." He threw the napkin on the table, towering in front of her. "One day, you will thank me for this."

"Fine." She lifted her chin. "I don't care. I warned you, my conscious is clear. If you want to die today, go ahead and answer that call in the mine."

Anger boiled in her blood, and golden sparks tingled her fingertips. Only years of training and practice of self-control guided her steps outside the lounge.

Once outside, blinded by fury, she ran toward her ship, fighting the tears pooled in her eyes.

Dammit. How many times is this guy going to make me cry? Memories from six years ago, when he humiliated her in front of everyone mixed with the unstoppable tears blurring her vision.

Only a few steps away from her ship, she recognized one of the bounty hunters plotting against Lord Tebbet. He paid some guards, then started toward the mine.

Caranna stopped and glanced at her ship, then back to the man walking in the opposite direction. Leaving, would mean she admitted herself defeated. Starting her career with a failure was not what she wanted or expected of herself.

What if I follow that guy and hide in the mine?

Maybe helping Lord Tebbet stay alive will convince him of who I am? Does it even matter? Yes, it does.

She lifted the hood of her duster, and covering her face as much as possible, she followed the bounty hunter toward the mine.

6

Tyren

THE UNDERGROUND WELCOMED him with the same clouds of glittering dust filling the air, as any other day. The call Caranna had told him he'd receive, came just as she had predicted.

Something seemed to have affected the unmoving line of shipping carts. Tyren let the energies gather around him, filling his being, and drawing the power he would need to face almost two dozen attackers. The six guards accompanying him every time he visited the mine, followed him closely.

Workers and soldiers continued to do their work, mining, supervising, or operating the machinery in the sparkling mine. The Brill crystals, stuck in the walls, appeared like minuscule shards of mirrors, reflecting the light. Unlike most mines, the underground in this case was brighter than the surface.

Tyren worked his way through the wide corridors, allowing invisible tendrils of energy to scout his surroundings. Fear and hate radiated from people hidden behind stacked crates, and he counted at least twelve.

Probably more ahead, he mused.

The large area hosting the main operation station came into view from around a corner. Each of his steps took him closer to a confrontation he knew wasn't going to be easy. Facing twenty or so attackers, even with his guards, was a stretch even for him.

A slight movement on one of the rafters floating about fifteen feet off the ground caught his eye. Whoever was up there, had just let him know he was surrounded, and fire would soon start pouring upon him from all directions, including from above.

The technician in charge with operating the panels straightened before him.

"My Lord." The man clicked his heels and bowed his head.

"What seems to be the problem?" Tyren closed

his hand around the hilt of his sword, the energies intensifying around him.

"I can't figure it out." Fear swirled around the middle-aged man. "I'll go check the cable box." The technician whirled and ran in the opposite direction.

The energies filled the space, danced, and snapped in the air with warnings of the imminent threat. On reflex, his hand tightened on his sword.

To his surprise, the guards were the first to make a move, pointing their rifles toward him.

"Traitors." He growled between clenched jaws.

From behind the stacked crates, more attackers came into view, the majority of them bounty hunters, and a few mercenaries.

She was right, this might be trouble. I didn't expect my own guards to turn against me.

Tyren activated his sword and the first of his invisible, protective shields. "Do you think there's enough of you?"

"Shut up, you smug bastard." One of the bounty hunters yelled, then nodded. "Open fire."

Before any charges left the business end of their rifles, a gold ribbon of light descended from the rafter where he'd seen movement only seconds ago. The tendril wrapped around his waist, expanded in a bubble, and yanked him in the air with nauseating speed and force.

The charges filled the air, converging to the spot he'd occupied until less than a second ago. His shoulder hit one of the stacked crates before he landed behind a couple of shipping containers.

"What in the stars?" He quickly recovered from the rough, unexpected landing, then lifted his gaze to the hand holding the golden threads. "You? What are you doing here?"

"Saving your ass. My Lord." Caranna ducked behind the containers now taking the onslaught of the rifles and blaster pistols firing in their direction.

"I thought I told you to leave." Tyren refused to admit aloud how grateful he was for her insubordination.

The betrayal of his own guards stung, boiling in his blood with anger.

"You're welcome." A smile parted her lips but didn't reach the chocolatey eyes he's never forgotten from years ago.

"I didn't ask for your help." Tyren cut the air with his sword. "You're going to get yourself killed."

He didn't want to be responsible for her death. By sending her away, Tyren tried to keep her safe.

Why did she have to be this stubborn?

"I know that you guardians have all sorts of defensive shields." She peeked to the men still firing their weapons from below. "Can you extend those shields to me?"

"In close—remarkably close—proximity, yes. What's your plan?" Tyren had to admit, her composure under pressure, was far superior to any newbies he'd seen in the past.

"If you keep me shielded, I'll take those guys out." She motioned to the other side of the containers they both used as cover.

"You can take them all out?" The question left his lips too soon, before he had the chance to revise his tone, and not sound so surprised.

"You're about to see me in action, My Lord. Taking out twenty targets in such a confined space, shouldn't take more than a minute or two." Golden lightning covered her arms, sparkling in her hands, as if eager to reach its next victim.

"I prefer to kill them myself." Tyren lifted his chin with pride. "And if you didn't yank me up here, I would've been half-way there by now."

"You'd be dead." Caranna snapped at him, then stood. "I don't care how mighty you think you are, that," she pointed to the firing weapons, "was a death sentence. Your own guards turned against you."

Dammit she's right. And I hate to admit it. He took a deep breath, using all the anger to feed his power.

"Fine." He stepped behind Caranna, one arm coiling around her waist. "Let's see what you can do." Tyren moved to the side with her, their steps in perfect sync.

"Tell me when your shield is active." Caranna's hands performed a dance in front of her, gathering energy, shaping it into a multitude of threads.

"Now." Tyren activated his first shield, pulling her out in the open, so she could have a clear line of sight.

The lightning shot from her hands filling the opening. Gold lines sparked in a chaotic pattern, never twice in the same spot, confusing the attackers scrambling for cover.

There was no hiding from the blitzkrieg of gold death delivered by the young woman he held close to him. Some of the lighting rotated, like the eye of a storm, midair, and forks hit the ground with explosions in the dirt or burned flesh when they struck their targets.

Shrieks and swearing mixed with the sound of the firing weapons, and the smell of burned flesh filled the air.

In only a few seconds, six bodies lay on the floor, and more groans of pain rose from the others. His first shield was about to expire, and Tyren switched to the next one, making sure he didn't leave both of them exposed.

One stray charge went through Caranna's shoulder.

"Urgh." Her arm lowered for a moment, only to rise back up.

"I'm sorry." Tyren stared at her crimson blood filling the hole left by the charge. "I had to activate another shield." He parried a charge with the blade of his sword, reflecting it back to its origin.

On the level below, one of the bounty hunters fell, shot by his own charge. The hole in his chest didn't even gave him a chance to welcome death with the familiar scream of fear.

With about half of the attackers dead already, the firing lessened. From the side, a mercenary fired a flurry of shots, one going through the protective shield.

Tyren clenched his teeth to stop a moan of pain. The charge burned a hole through his thigh, and his arm—the one closed around Caranna's waist —twitched.

"Looks like your shields are not completely safe." She glanced at his wound. "Can you heal yourself?"

"No." He shook his head. "But my regeneration rate is pretty high." Tyren checked on her wound, and the bleeding seemed to slow to a near stop. "And it seems yours is too."

"Yes, it is. Take us behind the container for a moment." Caranna side glanced at him, tiny beads of sweat lining her forehead.

With one step to the side, Tyren dragged her behind the improvised cover, but continued to hold her close to him. "Everything all right? Are you running low on energy?"

She shook her head. "No, but that shot is distracting me." She reached to her belt and pulled a small canister of kovor, spraying some of it on her shoulder. A thin, bluish layer of goo covered her wound. "Here," she handed it to him. "You should use some, too."

"I'm fine. It's just a scratch." He refused the kovor. A part of him, the one dominated by pride, pushed him to fight through the pain.

Caranna stared at him for a couple of seconds, then a smirk traveled from her lips to her eyes. "Tough guy, huh? Use it." She pushed the kovor in his hand. "I don't want you to bleed all over my brand-new leather suit."

If she saw through him, she kept it to herself, her reasoning convincing him to spray the remaining healing solution on his wound. The cooling gel numbed the burning spot, and he let out a silent sigh of relief.

"Are you happy now?" He threw the empty canister to their feet.

"No, but I might be when we're done here. How are those shields coming off cooldown?" Her hands gathered more of the gold lightning, preparing for round two.

"We're good. Are you ready?" Tyren activated the strongest shield in his arsenal. He didn't want her, or himself, to get hurt any further.

Caranna nodded, and he stepped to the side again, holding her tensed body against his, allowing the shield to close around both of them.

The energy coursing through her body, stronger than he'd ever sensed before from anyone else, took his breath away. Her command of destructive, obliterating attacks forced Tyren to admit the truth.

She is magnificent.

Gold strikes played in the air, chased, snapped,

and hit their targets. A few seconds later, the firing stopped.

"Looks like we're in the clear." He unwound his arm from around her waist, taking a step to the side, to see the area below them.

"No." She shook her head, her body still tense. "There are two more. I can sense them." More lightning took shape between her hands, but this time, she didn't release it in the air, instead, she held it like deadly whips.

Focused on maintaining the shields around them, Tyren hadn't kept tabs on his attackers. He quickly scouted the area with his senses.

"One is behind that stack." He pointed to a few crates on top of each other, near the main control station.

"And one more to his left." Caranna released two gold threads, aimed to the last two survivors.

The crates hiding them exploded form the powerful shocks, the Brill minerals stored inside pouring to the ground, and more dust filling the air. Her targets, the two men, walked from behind them, as if running away from the lighting following them.

Caught in the gold threads, their screams echoed in the mine, then they fell to the ground. Their lifeless bodies joined the others, now covered in a glittering dust.

"I have to admit." Tyren faced her. "I am impressed."

Caranna let the golden energy melt into her skin, her shoulders relaxing.

"Thank you, My Lord." She covered her chest with an open palm, slightly bowing her head. "When Professor Garnik sent me here, he didn't just assign you an average graduate."

"No, he did not." Tyren jumped on top of the one shipping container placed under the rafter, then hopped to the ground. "Come. We both need to go to the medical station." He favored his other leg, the injury suffered earlier still bothering him.

Caranna preferred to use the stairs and joined him in the middle of the bodies littering the ground.

"I can't believe my own guards betrayed me." He kneeled by one of the dead soldiers, removing his closed helmet. "I have handpicked every one of them, and this one is not one of my guards." Tyren rushed to the rest of his guards, pulling off their head gear. "None of them are."

"So where are your soldiers, then? Are you sure you would recognize them?" She drew near.

"One of the most basic rules for all my soldiers is

proper hygiene and grooming." He pointed to a man with an overgrown beard. "These men look like they haven't visited a barber in months." Tyren straightened and dialed a frequency.

His assistant, Lieutenant Sargon, answered on the first ring. "My Lord."

"There had been an ambush in the mine, by the main control station. The men inside my guards' armors are not the soldiers that should've been, but mercenaries. Find my guards and make sure they're all right."

"Right away, My Lord."

"And send someone to clean up the mess. There are over twenty bodies littering the station."

The lieutenant's eyes rounded, ready to pop out of their sockets. "Another attempt on your life, My Lord? Should I dispatch some troops?"

"Another *failed* attempt, yes." Tyren glanced at Caranna. She checked, making sure the attackers were indeed, all dead. "No need for troops. Sorceress Baro made quick work of them."

Without another word, Tyren terminated the connection.

"They are all dead. Now, we're in the clear." She faced him.

He focused on her face and tried to detect any

trace of deception in her eyes. Nothing. She'd been honest all along, and her determination made him question his own decision.

Maybe, it's time for the last of the tests.

"Would you die for me?" He asked the question, taking a step closer to Caranna.

As if to prove him wrong, again, she didn't answer right away. A thin line marked her forehead, and she bit her lower lip.

"Right now. . ." Caranna hesitated for a split second, then confronted him. "No." She squared her shoulders. "I don't know you well enough to lay my life at your feet. But I respect you enough to do my best and eliminate any threat. I'd keep dying as a last resort."

Tyren nodded, and a smile tugged at the corner of his mouth.

"That answer just earned you a mentor." He puffed his chest. "If you still want to be my apprentice, of course."

Pure joy erupted from her, and sparks animated her eyes.

"Are you serious? I thought you hated me." Confusion washed over her, like a thin veil.

"I never did, but I doubted your motives." Tyren gestured toward the exit in an invitation for her to walk with him. "If you'd said you would die for me, a lie, I would've never accepted you as my apprentice. You proved your honesty, and I appreciate it more than anything else."

"So, you don't want me to leave anymore?" She fell in step by his side.

"No. Starting this moment, you're my apprentice."

A shift, deep inside him, let him know it was the moment when his whole existence had changed direction.

I guess the future will tell if it was the right direction, or the wrong one.

7

Caranna

THE NEXT MORNING, Caranna scanned her bracer in front of the panel, and the doors to the lounge slid open. With the first step inside, the aroma of fresh coffee and tea mingled in the air with the smell of toast and mouthwatering fresh baked pastries.

From the same table as the previous day, Lord Tebbet stood and signaled her to approach.

Like he needed to do that, she wiped her hands on her hips. *Nobody can miss him in a room.*

Chin high, Caranna took in a deep breath and walked toward her mentor. It still felt like a dream about to come true. A mentor meant training, getting ready for her upcoming lordship trials, and to be that much closer to the recognition she craved.

With one step to the side of the table, Lord Tebbet pulled out a chair for her.

"Good morning, My Lord." She tilted her head with respect. "Thank you." Caranna sat, waiting for him to return to his seat.

Hm. Yesterday, he all but kicked me out. Nice to see some manners for a change.

"I hope you're rested." Her mentor placed the black napkin on his lap and reached for his steaming coffee. "Are your living arrangements and clearance resolved?"

"Yes. Lieutenant Sargon was extremely helpful yesterday." She grabbed her own napkin. "I understand your guards are safe?"

"Yes, they are. They found them stripped from their armors, tied, and soundly asleep with a couple of gas canisters in their dormitory." He sipped form his coffee. "At least they didn't turn on me as I had thought."

"That's good news." Caranna glanced around, unsure if she had to wait for a waiter, or let someone know she was a regular now.

"I wasn't sure what you would like, so I didn't

order anything for you." Lord Tebbet lifted a hand, and a waiter ran to their table.

"Good morning." The young man bent forward. "What would you like for breakfast, Miss?"

"Sorceress Caranna Baro is my new apprentice." Lord Tebbet's voice hardened, as if he wanted to make a point and put the waiter in place.

"I apologize, My Lord." The poor guy's eyes rounded with fear, then he faced her again. "Lady Baro."

Lady Baro. I like the sound of it, she mused.

"Not quite there yet but working on it." She smiled at the frightened waiter. "I'd like some tea, and whatever it is that smells so delicious."

"There's a new batch of croissants fresh out of the oven." The waiter's timid smile reminded her how non-energy users were always intimidated by her kind. Not to mention the presence of Lord Tebbet.

"Perfect. I'll have one of those." She leaned back in her chair.

"Would you like some chocolate with it? Or some nuts?" The young server pressed a couple of buttons on his data pad.

"Yes, and yes please."

"Right away, My Lady." The waiter left as quickly as he had appeared.

"I suggest you eat well. After breakfast, we'll start your training." Lord Tebbet leaned forward. "Did you bring your sword?"

"Yes." Caranna grabbed the hilt of her father's sword from under the folds of her duster. "As for breakfast, usually a cup of tea and an occasional slice of toast are enough to keep me going until lunch."

"Where did you get your sword?" A deep crease marked his forehead.

"It used to belong to my father. It's all I have left of him." Caranna tightened her hold around the intricate hilt.

"No wonder you had such a challenging time with it. Did nobody tell you it's completely wrong for you?" He reached for the weapon.

"Why is it wrong?" She placed the hilt in the palm of his outstretched hand.

"It's too big. This is a man's sword." He wrapped his hand around the hilt. "It is small for me, since I have larger hands, but at the same time, it's way too big for you." He turned his hand upside down. "You see, when you hold it, the tip of your thumb needs to barely touch your middle finger."

Caranna watched his thumb going over the tip of

his middle finger. She had no idea that swords had certain sizes, other than personal preference.

"Hold it." Lord Tebbet returned to her the hilt of her father's sword.

Her hand wrapped around the cold metal. There was about an inch gap between her thumb and middle finger. "I see what you're saying now."

"I'm surprised no one at the academy told you." He leaned back in his seat, allowing the waiter to place the breakfast on the table.

"When I wasn't getting anywhere with the weapons training, I quit it and took extra classes in energy use." She tucked the heavy hilt under her duster. "I tried at the beginning of each year, but the results were always the same."

"That was a bad move." He sipped again from his coffee. "While I can appreciate the sentimental value of your father's sword, you need your own. After we're done here, we'll stop by the armory."

Caranna picked a tea satchel and dropped it in her cup filled with hot water. "All right."

"Starting today, you will not leave my side unless I tell you to." He grabbed his fork and knife. "As my apprentice, you will observe everything. Keep your eyes and ears open. If you ever have questions, don't be shy about asking."

"Yes, My Lord." She swirled the teaspoon in her cup.

"We will travel together, unless there is a good reason to be on different ships or worlds." Lord Tebbet continued with the new rules.

Damn, I'll be on a short leash. But I guess there is a price to pay for my dream.

"All right." She closed her hands around the hot cup.

"With less than a year until the trials, you will need to train every day. If for whatever reason that won't be possible, you will have to make up for it the next day." He lifted his gaze to hers. "You will do what I tell you without arguing. I know what you need to do to pass those trials, and to be prepared for a lifetime of survival."

Caranna nodded, swallowing the first sip from her tea. The hot, aromatic drink exploded in her mouth with a bitter-sweet taste.

"You won't negotiate my orders but execute them. Are we clear so far?" Lord Tebbet took a mouth full of his scrambled eggs and meat.

Wow. Bossy much?

"Yes, My Lord." She broke a small piece of her croissant and dipped it in the melted chocolate.

"You will get time to rest and study, but personal

time off is not something I encourage." He paused for a few seconds, chewing, and swallowing his food. "You may contact your family and friends and let them know that you won't see them until after the trials."

"I have no family left, and no friends. But I will let my maid, Fira, know." Caranna grabbed a couple of the roasted almonds.

"You have a maid?" His surprise filled the air between them.

"Yes. She's taking care of my home." Caranna popped the almonds in her mouth. The crunchy nuts delighted her taste buds. "She used to be a slave, but I freed her, and she chose to stay with me."

"Interesting." He arched a brow and continued eating his breakfast.

"Even if Fira is only about five, or six years older than me, she's been everything from my nanny to my bodyguard, to my best friend. My great grandmother, who raised me since I was only a few months old, bought her for me when I was little."

"You may call her in your free time if the need arises, but I don't want anything to distract your focus from training." Lord Tebbet stared at her with an intensity which made her uncomfortable. "And that applies for boyfriends too. Understood?"

Caranna hurried to nod. "Yes, My Lord."

Boyfriends, she mused. *Like anyone would want to have a relationship with me.*

From hard learned lessons, Caranna knew how men only considered her attractive enough to spend a night with, but not good enough to take home.

After breakfast and a quick stop at the armory, with her new sword in hand, she followed Lord Tebbet toward the shuttle waiting with the engines roaring.

"Where are we going?" She boarded, sat, and clicked the safety harness.

"I figured, at least for now, you would prefer to train out of everyone's view." He lifted a hand, motioning to the pilot to take off. "You wouldn't want all the soldiers to know you can't hold a sword properly, would you?"

She shook her head, lowering her gaze to the tips of her boots.

"Lesson number one. Never let the enemy see you bleed, or your allies know your weaknesses." His deep voice reverberated over the noise of the engines.

"But you will." She turned to face him.

"We will spend a lot of time together. The relationship between an apprentice and his or her mentor is different." He narrowed his eyes to golden slits. "It takes a lot of trust. Both ways."

Caranna lowered her head.

Do I trust him? In battle when he extended his shield, it was as much for him as for me.

She hoped he would teach her everything she needed to know, but if it came to it, would she trust him with her life?

"Do you have an issue with trust?" His question caught her off guard.

Did he know what she was thinking?

"I've been betrayed in the past, and I guess I'm hesitant to trust anyone anymore." Memories from a few years back rose in her mind.

The one friend she thought she had and could rely on had turned against her, and the boy she thought she loved at the time, ended up dumping her all in favor of the same so-called friend. The double hit to her confidence wasn't something she could just forget about.

"Me too. And betrayal is something I can't overlook." Lord Tebbet clasped his hands together. "I can deal with the truth no matter how harsh, but never, ever, lie to me." He stared at her.

"I won't, My Lord." Caranna hurried to clarify her position.

The shuttle tilted to the side, and she glanced outside the window. The glittering snow-like effect was now absent, and forests covered the hills and valleys for as far as she could see. Bright dots of pink stood out against the lush green.

"It is beautiful." The whisper left her lips without consent.

Ugh. He's going to think I'm soft and weak.

Instead, a small smile tugged at the corner of his mouth. "It is. This planet is not only favored by the energies, but it's also home to magnificent views." He shifted on his seat. "May I call you Cara, when we're not in public?"

His unexpected question made her smile. "Of course, My Lord. My great grandmother used to call me Cara."

"When it's just the two of us, you may call me Tyren." His voice lowered, and for some reason, the air between them thickened with tension. "Or Ty, if you prefer."

"That would be disrespectful." She straightened her back.

Is he testing me?

"Respect, given or earned, is a lot more than a title."

The shuttle landed, concluding their discussion.

With a yank, Lord Tebbet opened the door by his side and exited, offering her a hand to help her out.

Caranna hesitated, but she didn't want to offend him in any way. Unused to someone—anyone—treating her with respect, as if she was more than just a nobody, both surprised and excited her.

She clicked off her harness and placed her hand in his.

"Caporal, you're off for the next three hours." He yelled at the pilot over the noise of the running engines.

"Thank you, My Lord. Do you want me to wait here, or come back in three hours?" The pilot appeared confused.

"Up to you." Lord Tebbet refocused his attention on her. "This way."

Each step by his side somehow, empowered her. Away from the busy base of operations, the essence of nature bloomed in rich colors. Beyond a line of tall trees blocking the view, a plateau welcomed her with a breathtaking show.

What she saw earlier from the shuttle as pink dots, turned out the be flowering trees. The branches were almost invisible, covered in full opened pink flowers. Not even the breather filtering the air could stop the sweet scent.

"It feels like we're on a different world. Are you sure we're still on Brillum?" She turned to face her mentor.

"Yes. This is one of my favorite places." He drew a wide arc in front of him. "I come here often to meditate."

A light breeze played in her hair. From above, thousands of pink petals danced in the air, floating on the soft winds and landing on the thick grass.

"Now, please take the first stance and activate your sword." Lord Tebbet's words broke the magic, yanking her back to reality.

8

Tyren

"You're as awkward as you were six years ago." Tyren shook his head.

Tension coiled around Caranna, and gold lightning sparked along the edges of her sword.

Her face scrunched in what would've been a funny expression, only her lack of connection with the weapon was nothing to laugh about.

"That," he pointed to the hilt of her sword, "is not just a weapon. It's your lifeline, an extension of your will to survive."

Caranna's hands tightened around the hilt until her knuckles turned white.

Tyren walked behind her, his left hand covering hers. "Breathe and relax."

Unlike the previous day, when he wore his armor, today he opted for his robe. The muscles on her back tensed even more against his chest.

"You connect with your sword through here," he gently tapped her right temple over the transparent shield covering her face. "Not through contact. You only have to hold your sword tight enough not to drop it, but loose enough to maneuver it."

A wave of heat radiated from her, and through the fabric of his robe, fastening his pulse.

His heart accelerated, a breath caught in his chest, and something snapped deep inside him, sending currents through his veins.

What in the stars?

With both his arms encircling her body, and his hands completely covering hers, Tyren noticed the goose bumps rising on her skin.

She feels it too. What is it?

He focused on the inner disturbance. A shock coursed his body, as if something had broken inside him, or something unknowingly broken had fixed itself, like a puzzle piece falling into place. The intensity nauseated him, the whole world spinning around.

Caranna turned her head to the side, staring at him. A light pink dusting covered her cheeks, under wide opened eyes. Her lips moved, but the loud roaring of his pulse drumming in his ears, made it impossible to hear anything.

Tyren took a step back, in an attempt to recover.

"My Lord, are you all right?" Finally, her words registered in his mind.

Caranna deactivated her weapon, grabbing his arm. Currents traveled from her, into his blood stream, igniting his being on fire.

"I need a minute." Out of breath, he hunched forward, propping his hands on his knees.

It seemed it was even harder to breathe doubled over, and he straightened.

Caranna took a step back, but waves of intense emotions swirled around her, distracting him further. If he didn't know better, they could've been mistaken for lust. But it was something more, something deeper, something more meaningful.

Time appeared to stretch, and he fought through each second, longer than the one before, to regain control over his raging inner self.

What is going on? What is this connection?

"My Lord? Shall I call for the shuttle?" Caranna's voice sounded sweet but overloaded with genuine concern. She grabbed his arm for a second time.

Tyren stared at her, as if he'd just seen her for the first time. A multitude of images flashed in his mind. Each one in an avalanche, rolling off of her with dizzying speed—the two of them together, fighting on a battlefield, getting married, holding a baby, smiling happy, tears, and pain. If they were a possible future, he couldn't say. One thing he was certain about, the images came to him from her, as if their minds had linked together.

Fear and confusion replaced all her other emotions, and she took a step back, on unsteady legs.

"No, I'm fine." His breath returned to normal. "Are you all right?"

Caranna shook her head. "What was that?" Her legs gave up on trying to support her body.

With a quick reflex, Tyren caught her, easing her onto the lush grass. "You are definitely not all right."

"What did you do to me?" One hand over her chest, she struggled to breathe.

"Nothing, I have no idea what it was." He sat beside her, himself in need of a break.

"It felt like a connection." Caranna shifted on the ground, facing him. "Is that how you connect with your apprentices?"

"No." Tyren pressed his hands on his temples, just beside the edge of his face shield. "This was a first."

She lowered her head. "Maybe it isn't a good idea for you to be my mentor." The words, just above a whisper, left her lips like a soft breeze.

"The images you saw, and somehow transmitted to me. . ." Tyren hesitated, but the need to know pushed him forward. "Were they visions of the future? *Our* future?"

Her shoulders moved up, then dropped back. "I don't know. I have never seen so many."

"What do you mean?" He wanted to grab her arm, shake the truth out of her, but controlled his urge.

"I've always seen images, usually one or two, disconnected. I never knew if they were visions or memories." She lifted her gaze to him. "Some turned out to have been visions, but they felt more like deja-vu. My great grandmother used to say that they might be memories from a previous life."

"How accurate were the ones turned to reality?" Tyren explored in his mind the possibility of the images reflecting a future together.

I don't mind it, but I am surprised about her being the one.

"Like I said, when I recognized them, they felt like memories."

"So, you're also gifted with visions. Why haven't you told me?" His brows drew near each other, suspicion slipping into his mind.

When she insisted to become his apprentice, did she know what would come of their relationship? Was she even attracted to him? The earlier faint hint of lust indicated in that direction. What about him? Could he see himself spending the rest of his life with her?

It would sure be interesting. She knows what she wants, and she's not shy about it. I like that about her.

"I didn't think it was important. Not to mention, I don't think I'm any good at it." Hesitance mixed with modesty in her voice. "I wouldn't count on any of those images to become true."

Tyren held back the question burning on the tip of his tongue. Did she want them to? Did he?

"The future will tell." He inhaled at full capacity of his lungs. "Are you ready to go back to your training?"

"No." She shook her head. "I have questions."

"Ask. This is why I'm here." He nodded toward her.

"Why do I need all this training? As a sorceress, I

will always use my connection with the energies, not a sword." Confusion reflected in her chocolatey eyes.

Tyren took a deep breath, letting it out slowly, and with it, the last remnants of the earlier disturbance. "Why do you want to take the lordship trials?"

"Is this a trick question?" She straightened her back, as if a hot iron had touched her spine. "I want my Dark Lady title."

"Why? What does that title mean?" Tyren narrowed his eyes, focusing on the young woman before him, the one with whom he could spend the rest of his life.

Not a terrible option at all.

"Recognition. Respect for my power." Chin high, she held his gaze.

"You don't need a title for those. Soon enough, people will learn your name, come to know what you're capable of." Tyren propped his arms on bent knees. "And you will make some enemies along the way. The higher you climb in ranks, the more you will have to watch your back."

"I am more confused now than before I asked the question." Caranna's shoulders dropped as if disappointment weighed heavy on them.

"It is all about survival, Cara." Tyren leaned

forward. "The trials will test your ability to survive in pretty much any circumstances. The title awarded to you means nothing more than a confirmation, a warning, if you want, that you are not an easy target."

"Survival?" She tilted her head to the side, her brows wrinkling on her smooth forehead. "I'm a pretty good sorceress, I can survive."

An involuntary smile tugged at the corner of his mouth. "Not if you can't connect to the energies, you can't."

Her eyes opened wider. "Why wouldn't I?"

"Because in reality, there might be circumstances that will stop you from doing that. Without the energies, you're vulnerable." Tyren reached for her hand, but she drew back and away from his touch.

Yeah. Considering what just happened a few minutes ago, I can't blame her.

"Give me an example of such circumstance." Doubt coated her words.

"Energy disrupting cuffs, electromagnetic fields, or even certain worlds where the energies are out of reach." Tyren leaned back, propping his hands on the soft grass behind him.

Realization seemed to slowly settle in her mind, her expression morphing from doubt to fear to determination.

"I see. Combat is something I should know, to fall back on if needed in situations like that." But it appeared she still had questions, and she leaned closer to him. "Why didn't anyone explain this to me in the academy?"

"Their job is to train you, make you the best you can be in your respective class." Tyren smiled, amused by her reactions. "It's not their obligation to make sure you'll stay alive. That is what the lordship training and trials are for."

"Now it makes sense." Caranna nodded. "So, you will teach me the swordsmanship I need to pass the trials?"

"That, and combat." Tyren brought a hand in front of him, his index finger pointing to her. "And it won't be just to pass the trials, but to serve you a lifetime, to keep you alive. This is my job as your mentor."

Without any warning, Caranna jumped to her feet. In the rush, one of her boots caught the edge of the long, ample duster she wore, causing it to split from the waist.

Tyren noticed the discreet attachments, holding the piece of clothing together, or apart, according to her preference.

"Now, I'm ready." She activated her sword.

His gaze roamed up her body, hidden until then by the long duster. Now with only the vest part of it left, he admired her long and soft lines, the grace replacing the earlier awkwardness in each of her movements.

She's going to do well.

9

Caranna

Two WEEKS LATER, Caranna walked by Tyren's side toward the Dark Citadel where she would witness a Dark Circle's meeting for the first time.

The towering building, the heart of the Grand Federation, took her breath away as it did in the past.

"I've imagined this moment for years." She blinked back the moisture from her eyes.

"You have never been in the Citadel before?" Tyren slowed his pace.

"Once." She nodded. "But it was one of those group visits, meant to inspire us."

"I remember those group activities. They are

mostly useless." Tyren tilted his head in response to a couple of people bowing their heads in front of him.

I so want that. People knowing who I am, showing me respect. And I'll get it one day. Soon.

"Why do you think they're useless?" She side-glanced at him. He looked as good as always, and recently, had become more and more attractive each day. "At least in my case it worked. I've always dreamed one day to walk through those front doors as a full-fledged sorceress."

"Visiting a building can be impressive, but mock-up missions, even live ones, would have a bigger impact in shaping young minds."

"A live mission?" Her tone scaled up in disbelief. "You would send a ten-year-old into battle?" Caranna stopped in the middle of the busy street.

"Of course not." Tyren continued to walk at a slower pace. "Not all missions involve fighting. Have those kids guard something, for instance, or retrieve something from a safe place."

Caranna hurried to catch up with him. "You can't expose children to danger like that." She stood her ground.

"Of course you can—supervised, and making sure the little ones don't get hurt." He glanced at her. "That would motivate them more, the sense of accomplishment would push them forward, and the bitter taste of failure teach them perseverance."

He even has the beliefs of a warrior. I wonder how he would raise his own children.

For a few moments, Caranna tried to imagine some of her flash-visions coming to life—an activity she'd indulged in almost every night since she'd met him, since the link between their minds had activated on Brillum. There, under the shower of pink flower petals, where she first had a glimpse into a possible future together, it was the first time she discovered the attraction toward him.

A silent sigh left her lips. The initial attraction only grew with each moment spent together with the man by her side.

From the first step on the bridge leading to the entrance in the Dark Citadel, she glanced over the edge. The multileveled city of Ori-Garr, Simran's capital, unraveled through thin fog floating in the air. Tall buildings, with tops disappearing into the clouds, continued below, like huge spears planted into the heart of the planet itself.

"I have noticed in the past couple of weeks that your connection with the energy is always flat." Tyren yanked her back to reality. "It should fluctuate when you draw on others' emotions."

"I don't." Caranna lowered her gaze to the square slabs of gray stone paving the high bridge.

How am I going to explain this one without admitting the truth?

"What do you mean?" He stopped in front of her. "It is the most basic combat technique."

"I've learned to only rely on myself. Feeling what others do, is not something I enjoy." Usually, evasion helped her with not talking about her past, but now she doubted it would work.

Tyren's eyes narrowed to thin golden slits, and he closed a hand on her arm. "What happened to you? Why did you cut yourself off from everyone?"

"We're going to be late." She tried to free herself from his firm hold. "We should go."

"The truth." His demanding growl sent shivers down her spine. "Now."

"Fine." Anger rose from inside, simmering under her skin. "You want to know why? I'll tell you why." Caranna yanked her arm free, closing her fists. "I have spent all those years in the academy bullied, pitied, overlooked, always left out. After a while, I got sick of feeling that same thing from everyone."

Tyren stared at her a few seconds, as if processing the information she'd just spit out.

"That's why you're so determined to get that

title." He resumed walking toward the citadel's entrance. "You want to prove them all wrong."

"You're damn right. Too bad the ones that hurt me most are not around anymore." Caranna inhaled a large gulp of the crisp, morning air in an attempt to calm herself.

"Who?" He stopped for a moment, waiting for her to catch up with him.

"The girl who I considered my friend, and the guy I once loved. Or at least I thought so." Sadness wrapped around her, as it did every time she remembered the past.

"Do you want to talk about them?"

"There's nothing left to say. He cheated on me with her, only to eventually dump me." With each word spoken, anger left her being.

"I see. What happened to them?" Tyren clasped his hands behind him.

Caranna side glanced at him, curious of his reaction. His stone-chiseled face lacked any expression.

"They died in a group mission."

"I thought those missions were supervised. The teachers are responsible for the students' lives." His tone revealed confusion.

"The two of them separated from the group so they could have some . . . Umm . . . Privacy. They got shot." Caranna relaxed her shoulders. Guilt had tortured her for months after their deaths, but now she knew it wasn't her fault.

"Were you in that mission, with them?"

Caranna shook her head. "No. As always, I wasn't included in those missions. I wasn't good enough." A tinge of pain stabbed her heart.

A loud sigh left his lips, and Caranna looked at him again. His brows had drawn closer to each other, a deep line separating them. "I don't understand. Your power didn't just appear overnight. Somebody must've sensed it."

"Actually, it did." Caranna glanced toward the city, then refocused on the man before her. "At the beginning of my fourth year in the Academy, my connection with the energies scaled up. In the first class with Professor Garnik I almost killed one of the other students."

"What do you mean?" Lord Tebbet seemed more and more interested.

"That student laughed at me, as usual, and I just lost it. Something inside me snapped and I attacked him, unaware of the surge of power." The memory, still vivid in her mind, had always been bitter-sweet. "Professor Garnik pulled me to the side, and since that day he trained me in private."

"What about the other professors?"

"At his recommendation, I hid my newly discovered power. I held back, and only let everyone see it at my graduation trials." She couldn't stop a chuckle. "You should've seen their faces. After all those years of being deemed weak and good for nothing, I finally showed them what I had become. It was worth it."

"I am sorry for what you have experienced in the academy, but now you've graduated. Leave the past behind and move on. Can you do that?" Tyren squared his shoulders.

She preferred not to answer, searching in her mind and in her heart for the resolution she needed. He was right.

"Now, more than ever, you need to be aware of others' emotions. Potential enemies will always lurk in the shadows." Tyren stepped off the bridge, and onto the large platform marking the grand entrance into the citadel.

"I will try." She lifted her gaze to the top of the pointed towers decorated with long and narrow windows.

From two of them, oversized banners bearing the federation emblem, hung on either side of the entrance. The red flame burning through a chain, contrasted with the black background, bringing a splash of color against the gray building.

"You will do more than try. While we are in the council room, you will scout the other's emotions." His firm tone didn't leave any room for objections. "At the end of the meeting, you will report to me. Are we clear?"

"Yes, My Lord."

"Good." He nodded and entered the citadel through the huge, opened doors flanked by guards on either side. "During the meeting you will stand to my left, inside the red circle. Other than you, there will be three more apprentices. You are the only woman."

Caranna nodded, following him through the vast entrance, and into one of the arched corridors leading to the elevators.

"You will not speak, unless asked to. Control your emotions and show everyone you deserve to be there." Tyren pressed a button and the elevator's doors swished open.

"I got it. Keep quiet and make note of everyone's emotions." Caranna stepped inside.

"Yes." Tyren pressed the lowest of the buttons. "The meetings are usually boring, so you won't miss much by not paying attention to the conversations." Both steel-brushed doors closed, and the elevator set in a fast descent. "But you will learn about the dynamics of the Dark Circle."

"Yes, My Lord." Caranna took in a deep breath, letting it out slowly, cleansing her body of all anger, guilt, and desire for retribution.

I am here, the only one in my class to already have a mentor. Everyone who ever doubted me can crawl under a rock and die.

Head held high, Caranna followed Tyren out of the elevator and toward the black, double doors leading to the council room.

Her pulse accelerated—a dream was about to come true. But inside each dream, there is a nightmare waiting to happen. And hers presented itself in the shape of one of the other apprentices—Khaon.

A couple of years older than her, Khaon was the one who gave her the nickname *Whitey.* She hated it, and the way it stayed with her all throughout the academy. Her only hope was that he wouldn't recognize her.

All the other dark lords and their apprentices stopped in the middle of their conversation, staring at her and Lord Tebbet.

I bet they can hear my heart beats, she mused in the dead silence filling the round room.

"Lord Tebbet." One of the dark lords took a step

forward from his green circle. "We heard rumors that you took a girl apprentice, but I see it's true.

Caranna knew all the names of the lords leading The Grand Federation, but at that moment, she couldn't remember any of them.

"Yes, it's true." Tyren nodded, then turned toward her. "My new apprentice, third class sorcerer, Caranna Baro." He continued his way to the red circle and sat in his chair.

Caranna felt like a hundred blades stuck in in her back at the same time. Even if she wanted to ignore all the hate, fear, and envy rising around her, she couldn't. She followed him and stood by his left side as he'd instructed her earlier.

"Third class? She's too young." Another lord leaned forward in his chair, his gaze measuring her, as if wanted to convince himself.

"Yes. You know the academy's rules." Tyren leaned against the backrest. "Third class is the highest they can award upon graduation. She's actually closer to first class."

Heads shook and murmurs replaced the silence from before. The other apprentices stared at her as if she'd grown an extra head.

"Is she the one who did that number on bounty hunters and mercenaries back on Brillum?" Another question rose from the unintelligible general whispering.

"Yes. I feel sorry for whoever financed that attempt on my life. I hope they didn't pay in advance." Her mentor appeared to have fun.

"Perhaps it was just luck." The dark lord who appeared to be Khaon's mentor waved a dismissive hand. "I'm willing to bet five thousand credits, that my apprentice can defeat her in less than a minute."

Caranna tensed. Was this how their meetings usually went, or was this an exception? Would Tyren throw her into combat with another apprentice to teach him a lesson, or for the credits?

Crimson sparks glowed around her mentor's hands when they grabbed on the armrests. "As much as I would enjoy seeing any of your *boys* humiliated, my apprentice is not here for anyone's amusement."

If she'd been anywhere else, she would've kissed him. Not that she hadn't fantasized about it, especially when she faked a wrong step, or a minor accident, just so he would hurry to catch and hold her in his arms. Caranna quickly pushed the attraction she felt toward him to the back of her mind.

"*Boys?*" Another dark lord sounded offended. "Should I remind you that my apprentice is only two years younger than you?"

Caranna glanced toward the apprentice in discussion—medium build, nothing special, he closed his hand around the hilt of his sword, as if ready to take on the challenge.

"And what does that tell you about him?" Tyren seemed to have an answer for everything. "If I were you, I wouldn't brag about it. He's either a slow learner, or simply not cut for it."

"Can we focus on today's topics?" The dark lord from inside the blue circle, Lord Raz Harett—to her surprise she remembered his name— interrupted the verbal sparring. He didn't have an apprentice by his side, and from what she could tell, there was no hate or envy radiating from him.

The meeting was boring, just as her mentor had warned her, and Caranna focused on the task he'd given her. Detecting all the others' emotions wasn't as hard as she expected it to be after years of not even attempting to do it.

She wanted him to be proud of her, of a job well done. Dealing with all the emotions flooding the room, was a different story. Especially the lust floating from two of the other apprentices and directed at her.

10

Tyren

"SHE IS DISRUPTING THE MEETING." Dark Lord Brode glanced at his apprentice, Khaon, then pointed an accusatory finger at Caranna.

"How is she doing that?" Tyren closed his fists, letting the crimson sparks dance around his knuckles. "She'd been standing here for over an hour without a word."

"She is distracting our apprentices." Dark Lord Dovor hurried to support his friend. At his side, his apprentice, Vitez, shifted his weight from one leg to the other.

Tyren knew from past experience that two of his

enemies always worked together, usually against him.

"Then maybe your *boys* should learn how to control their lust." Tyren had sensed the young apprentices' poor management of their emotions earlier, and wanted to blast them with energy, or at least call them out.

How dare they lust over Caranna.

The two dark lords glanced at each other, lips tight, and visibly unsatisfied with his answer.

"She should leave the room and wait for you outside." The third wheel of the ongoing clique, Dark Lord Gowon, leaned in his chair. At least his apprentice, Pollex, had a better control of his emotions.

"No." Tyren fought the impulse of challenging everyone in the room and end the politics game. "My apprentice has the exact same rights as yours. If they stay, she does too."

He regretted his words as soon as they came out. The last thing he wanted was to throw Caranna by herself against all three other apprentices. Not he doubted she could stand her own, but he didn't want to give the others the satisfaction of seeing her in action.

The trio of dark lords united against him nodded

at each other. "So be it. They'll wait outside for these last few minutes of our meeting." Lord Brode waved a dismissive hand at his apprentice, quickly followed by the others.

With a deep breath, he turned to Caranna. "Please wait for me outside." He had to keep a casual appearance, when inside all his being revolted.

"Yes, My Lord." Caranna bowed her head, then started to the exit, following the other apprentices out of the room.

I so want her to teach them a lesson. Hopefully, she'll remember her training.

"It is our understanding, that despite all the events on Brillum, you managed to recover and surpass the deficit in Brill crystals?" Lord Gowon refocused on him as soon as the double doors closed.

"Yes. Your informants did their job well." Tyren couldn't help taking a jab at the other dark lord. "Perhaps they deserve a raise?"

For one short moment he enjoyed the discomfort rising from the other man, but a fluctuation in the energies, on the other side of the door attracted his attention. Focusing, he noticed Caranna's distress.

"You can't blame any of us for using informants." Lord Dovor lifted his pointy chin. "You have them, too."

Tyren stood. "Something is happening out there." He motioned to the door, then pressed a few buttons on the built-in commands of his chair.

A large screen flickered to life in the middle of the room, and images from the other side of the closed doors came to life.

"Do they know there are cameras in the antechamber?" Dark Lord Harett, quiet until then, leaned forward.

"My apprentice doesn't." Tyren drew closer to the moving images showing Caranna surrounded by the other three.

One by one, the other three mentors shook their heads.

"When I heard your name, I thought it sounded familiar." Khaon advanced closer to Caranna.

"Really? I'm surprised since you never used it." She retreated, but golden threads gathered around her hands.

"C'mon, Whitey was so much more appropriate." The apprentice who seemed to have been one of her tormentors in the academy, gathered energy around him. "But look at you now." He laughed. "You really are the swan who merged from an ugly duckling."

The other two apprentices must've found it

funny, and their laughs filled Tyren's ears with an insulting sound.

"Look, she's all sparkling." Vitez activated his two swords, cutting two circles in the air.

"Wait. Maybe we can have some fun before we teach her where her place is." Khaon drew near Caranna. "What do you say, pretty? Should we *spark* together?"

Caranna's shoulders tensed, and the golden ribbons around her hands dimmed their glow.

She's not buying that load of crap. Is she? Tyren closed his hands into fists, ready to throw all caution to the wind and run to her side.

"Maybe." Caranna took a step closer to Khaon. "But I don't even know all your names." She glanced at the other two.

"This is Vitez," Khaon nodded to his right. "And this is Pollex." He pointed to his left.

"Nice meeting you." Caranna's words, oversaturated with fake sweetness, left no doubt she would've rather not.

"So," Khaon prodded further. "How about losing some of your leather?"

"You should know, I have an extremely sensitive nose. Smells affect my mood." She winked at the three apprentices moving too close to her.

"What, you want to sniff me before we have some fun?" Khaon's luminous ribbons glowed brighter. "Here."

With only a couple of inches between him and Caranna, she placed her hands on his shoulders, and inhaled close to the side of his neck.

"Just as I thought. You do smell. . ." a wide smile parted her lips "like a rat."

Her hands tightened on the young man's shoulders, and her knee rushed into his lower ribs. Khaon bent over with a groan of pain, and she jammed her elbow in his face, sending him to the ground.

'Atta girl. She didn't forget what I taught her. Tyren's heart swelled with pride.

Only Vitez, the apprentice with two swords, managed to slash her right arm, through the long glove riding close to her shoulder. Blood filled the gash, and the golden threads around her hands shaped into a wall, pushing back all three of her opponents.

The wave of energy, released with all the anger and hate reflected in her eyes, sent the assailants flying backwards, slamming them into and through the doors.

Tyren moved his gaze from the screen to the wide

opened doors just in time to see two of the apprentices landing on their rears, in the middle of the council's room. The third one, came too close to the black marble floor, hitting his head on the hard surface.

I so want to kiss her right now.

He squared his shoulders, shifting his attention toward Caranna.

"Looks like you should've taken him on that bet." Lord Raz Harett chuckled.

The three mentors stared with disbelief at their defeated apprentices.

Guilt and fear swirled around Caranna, mixing with the rush of adrenaline washing off of her after the short, but so satisfying fight.

"Are you all right?" Tyren motioned her to approach.

"Yes, My Lord." Caranna stopped in front of him, trying to hide the bleeding cut. "I apologize for the interruption." She lowered her head.

"You're injured." Tyren grabbed her arm, causing her to wince.

"It's not bad, just a scratch." She braved, despite the sharp intake of air.

"He hit his head on that rough landing." Lord Dovor checked on Pollex, the one lying unconscious on the floor, then rose to his feet. "He'll wake up, eventually."

Khaon finally rose from the floor, his face covered in blood from what appeared to be a broken nose. "You bitch," he spat.

Caranna's anger escalated again, but only for a fraction of a second, followed by a cold calm. "Do you remember Whitey?" Satisfaction filled her being, radiating from her with the power of a thousand suns. "She just kicked your sorry ass."

Tyren covered the lower half of his face with an open palm to hide the smile he couldn't control.

"And you," Caranna faced the apprentice placing his two swords on his belt. "You owe me a new pair of gloves." She pointed to the ruined glove on her right arm, soaked in blood.

"Let's take you to the medical bay." Tyren had to say something, to stop himself from laughing. "We don't want you to bleed all over the place."

"Yes. Khaon, you should see a medic as well." His mentor, Lord Brode clasped a hand on his apprentice's shoulder.

"Looks like you'll have to carry yours, Lord Gowon." Tyren pointed to the still unconscious apprentice on the floor.

More hate rose from the dark lords who had

made a mission from keep sending people to kill him and failing. Every. Single. Time.

With a short nod, Tyren walked out of the council room with Caranna by his side.

"I have never felt this proud in my life." He whispered to her as soon as they were far enough from the other lords.

"You're not mad at me?" Genuine surprise sparked in her chocolatey eyes.

"Not at all." He shook his head, leading her through the next corridor toward the medical bay. "Those little pricks got what they deserved. And you applied everything I taught you flawlessly. Well done."

A shy smile parted her lips. "At first, I didn't think I could take all of them, but then I remembered what you told me about distracting an opponent who otherwise would overpower me."

"Never forget that." Tyren smiled. "One day, it might save your life, or the ones you love."

"I'll keep it in mind."

"And next time, you'll have to kill them." Tyren whispered into her ear.

"Next time?"

"Enemies never turn into friends. If they came after you once, they'll do it again, and it's safer to not give them another chance." He pushed open the door to the medical bay. "After we're done here, we'll go have lunch. You deserve a celebration."

"Thank you, My Lord."

"I need a healer." Tyren walked toward a group of nurses.

"Yes, My Lord." A young woman hurried to Caranna. "I'm a healer." Her warm, yet confident smile, assured Tyren that Caranna was in good hands. The lavender aura surrounding the woman felt calming. "This way." She pulled to the side one of the curtains and helped his apprentice sit on the hospital bed.

From behind him, a little girl, no more than five years old, ran past him and to the side of the healer.

"What is she doing here? This is not a childcare." Tyren meant to sound firm, but the little girl's hands started to glow in the same shade of lavender.

"This is my daughter, Riata. She's going to the academy next year, but she's already manifesting incredible healing power." The mother smiled at her daughter. "I have all the clearance for her. She'll be observing."

"Make sure my apprentice won't have a scar." Tyren struggled to keep a serious tone in front of the sweet smile the girl displayed. One of her front teeth was missing.

"Of course, My Lord." The healer set to work, and the small space lit up in lavender shades, glowing ribbons flowing from her fingertips and wrapping around Caranna's arm. "You may wait outside, in the lounge. It's more comfortable."

One hour later, without any scar on her arm, Caranna walked out of the medical bay waving back to the smiling little girl.

"Ready for lunch?" Tyren closed the two screens floating above his bracer, then stood from the chair he'd been sitting on.

"Ready." Caranna nodded. "That girl is going to be a great healer one day."

"Good. We can never have too many of those." Tyren glanced back at the girl. Her toothless smile melted his heart.

I can't wait to have one of my own, he mused.

11

Caranna

AFTER LUNCH at the upscale restaurant, she started toward the exit by Tyren's side, but a waiter hurried to them.

"My Lord," the man bowed so low, Caranna thought he would hit his head on the nearest table. "There's been an incident, and until we clean up, please use the exit through the patio area."

"Very well." Tyren turned to her. "This way." One of his hands touched her back for a moment, to direct her toward the wall of windows.

Just like every prior time, his touch sent tingles

through her body, and her spine straightened, tension fusing each of her vertebrae to the next.

Outside, the noise of the lively city filled her ears. Tables under huge umbrellas lined the long patio.

"Tyren?" A woman's surprised voice came from her right.

I hope we didn't just run into some jealous girl-friend. I'm getting tired of explaining myself to everyone.

Her mentor froze in place, then smiled. "Mother."

Mother? Not a girlfriend, good.

Caranna looked at the woman holding a teacup near her lips. With her pinky up in the air, she stared at the man beside her with round, green eyes, from under a fancy, oversized white hat.

"Why didn't you tell me you were coming home?" She lowered the cup placing it on the delicate saucer. "This is a delightful surprise."

Tyren bent over and kissed his mother's cheek. "We only arrived three days ago."

"We?" His mother's emerald eyes turned to Caranna.

"Yes. This is my new apprentice, sorceress

Caranna Baro." Tyren smiled at her. "Cara, this is my mother, Lady Vione Tebbet."

"Vione Tebbet-Sterek." His mother's correction thickened the air with tension. "I'm a proud descendent of Sterek House." The smile parting her lips didn't reach her eyes.

"It's an honor, My Lady." Caranna bowed her head, fighting the uneasiness slipping into her bones.

"Baro." The older woman gestured to her and Tyren to sit. "I don't think I know your family."

Tyren held out a chair for her, and Caranna sat on the edge of it.

"You wouldn't, My Lady." Caranna forced a smile. "I was born on the world of Turron."

"I have to admit, I don't know much about your world." Tyren's mother glanced toward her son, then back at her. "Is your family part of nobility, in this world?"

"Not by the standards you have here on Simran." Caranna shifted on the edge of her chair.

She let timid tendrils of energy wrap around the other woman, searching for her emotions. The reality shouldn't have surprised her, yet she couldn't help the hurt stabbing her heart.

This lady doesn't even know me, yet she already hates me.

"Oh? What do you mean?" Lady Vione sipped from her tea. "Would you like a tea, dear? Or do you also drink that disgusting coffee, like Tyren?"

"We just had lunch, Mother." Tyren's tone carried the same tension as his mother's.

"Lunch?" She checked the time. "This late?"

"Yes." Her mentor let out a sigh. "The Dark Circle's meeting and the events following it, took longer than expected."

"How distasteful." His mother picked a perfectly round, bite sized cookie. "Those lords of yours have no notion of time. Civilized people take breaks for lunch." She refocused on Caranna. "You were telling me about your world's nobility." Lady Vione placed the cookie in her mouth, and started chewing it slowly, as if she calculated every single movement.

Not that it would make any difference. She already thinks I'm a low-life.

"A family's good name and reputation is related to how many energy users that family had given the galaxy." Caranna tried her best to sugar coat the much sharper answer in her mind.

She would've like to tell the woman in front of her that nobility is not carried by blood, but by one's actions.

"And who leads your people, the family with the

most children?" Disgust coated the older woman's words, and terror reflected in her eyes.

"No, the leaders are elected from the wisest ones, from the people with the most accomplishments, from—"

"How barbaric." Lady Vione placed a hand on her chest, over the green silk blouse. "A whole world of . . ." she paused, as if searching for the right word. "*Commoners.*"

Caranna was used to being labeled, but the way Tyren's mother voiced her opinion, rubbed her the wrong way. An insult, even if disguised as a clash of cultures, was still an insult.

"Mother." Tyren's voice rose just about a whisper. "She is a powerful sorceress, and soon to be a Dark Lady. You can't go around throwing labels like that."

And again, he stands up for me. This is going to take time to get used to. Caranna's attraction for her mentor expanded, filling her whole being.

"What? It's true—all that I've said." His mother's offended tone would've been funny if she hadn't just insulted a whole planet.

"We should go." Tyren stood, fists closed by his sides. "Caranna has a training session in a few minutes." He held her chair, pulling it back as soon as she rose to her feet.

Lady Vione tilted her head back, and her emerald eyes narrowed to think slits. "And how long have you two been sleeping together?"

Caranna drew in a sharp breath, and at her side, Tyren's shoulders stiffened.

"Mother. She is my apprentice." Indignation radiated from him in waves.

"Please." His mother waved a dismissive hand. "I may not like your kind, the energy users, but I'm not stupid. An apprentice walks behind his, or her mentor, not in front or beside him." Lady Vione lifted her chin, as if proud of her knowledge.

"My Lady." Caranna found her voice. "I assure you, our relationship is strictly—"

"And she talks out of turn, without permission." His mother pointed an accusatory finger at him. "You can't fool me."

Something snapped inside Caranna, her brain shut off and her instincts took over. After the earlier events, and a life-long string of humiliation, insults, and dismissal, she had had enough.

With a complicit smile, she turned to Tyren.

"I think is only fair that at least your mother

knows the truth." Casually, she placed a hand on his chest. His heart beats accelerated under her palm, and Caranna lifted herself on her toes. "No sense in hiding it."

Her other hand wrapped around his neck, and she pulled him toward her, pressing her lips to his.

Rejection was familiar ground for her, and she expected Tyren to push her away. Only he drew her closer, crushing her against his body, and deepening the kiss.

The whole world disappeared, and she let herself be carried away by instinct, attraction, and a fantasy which dominated her mind ever since she'd had the flash visions.

"Oh my." Lady Vione's gasp brought her back to reality, and she broke the kiss.

"Now, if you will excuse us, Mother." Tyren kept one arm coiled around her waist. "We have a training session waiting for us." With a short nod, he turned his back to his mother, holding her close to him. "Shall we?" His gold eyes bored through her soul.

"It was a pleasure meeting you, My Lady." Caranna smiled over a shoulder, in his mother's direction.

The older woman, close to fainting, fanned herself with a napkin.

She might have ruined everything, and if Lord Tebbet dismissed her from being his apprentice, she couldn't blame him. This was definitely not how an apprentice-mentor relation worked.

What have I done?

12

Tyren

"WOULD YOU LIKE A DRINK?" In his home office, Tyren poured about an inch of hard liquor in a crystal glass. His hands still shook.

Ever since Caranna kissed him in the middle of the restaurant's patio, he'd fought his instincts. Her kiss shattered his soul into ten solar systems and ignited his being on fire.

No woman had ever had such an impact on him. Usually, it took more than an innocent kiss in public to even catch his attention. Yet, Caranna had broken him, ruined the collected man he used to be.

Tension built between them, like a thick web ready to blow to pieces.

"No, thank you." She closed the door behind her. "I'm sorry for—"

"I have to apologize for my mother's behavior." He finally faced her and took a mouthful from the amber liquor in the glass.

Tyren refused to talk to her on the way home, rejecting her attempt at an apology. He needed all his focus inward, to stop himself from acting on instinct.

Why did she kiss him? Was it solely to teach his mother a well-deserved lesson? Or had she finally decided to follow through with the lust he'd sensed radiating from her over the past couple of weeks? A multitude of questions filled his mind, fighting each other to come out.

Could he let instincts guide him this time? If he did, how would it affect their relationship?

For the love of stars, I'm her mentor.

"What were you thinking?" Tyren drained the rest of the amber liquid and placed the empty glass on the tray. He hoped the fiery drink would burn all the questions away, but it only left a trail of lava down his throat.

Head lowered, Caranna stopped in the middle of the room.

"I wasn't, really—thinking that is." She shrugged. "Today, I've heard one too many insults, I guess. I just snapped." Her words echoed just above a whisper.

In two long strides, Tyren closed the distance between them. His hands ached to touch her, and he closed his fists in an attempt to control his urges.

"You just snapped?" Despite his drumming pulse, and struggling to remain calm, he kept a low tone. "And that was your best go to?"

"I . . ." Caranna lifted her gaze to him. The chocolate-colored irises revealed fear, guilt, and defiance all mixed together. "I don't know what came over me. It was unprofessional and if you want to drop me as your apprentice, I understand."

Her fear and sadness hurt him, it made it unbearable in the room.

"There is only one problem with what you've done." Tyren inhaled a gulp of air.

"Only one?" A flicker of hope sparked in her eyes.

"I want more." Left hand closed on the back of her head, Tyren drew Caranna closer, his lips crashing over hers.

Her hesitation only lasted for a moment, then she kissed him back with a passion matching his.

The pieces of his soul found their way back to him, gathering, yet not ready to glue back together. Something was missing. Could've been his own guilt —the feeling of letting down his apprentice—or not knowing her motives?

Out of air, she broke the kiss.

Tyren leaned his forehead against hers. "I hope you are not doing this because I'm your mentor and you feel you can't say no to me."

Caranna drew back a couple of inches, lifting her dark gaze to him. "Trust me, I have no problem saying no to you."

A smile tugged at the corner of his mouth. Yes, he had to agree with her. She had no issues when it came to standing up for herself against anyone, him included.

"If we go down this path, there won't be a way back." Tyren slid his hand from the back of her head to the side of her face.

With a slight tilt of her head, she gently pressed into the palm of his hand. "I don't think there ever was one."

"Cara," Tyren gently ran his thumb over her lips.

"I am not sure I can stop once I give into my attraction for you."

Her arms glided up his shoulders, then closed around his neck. "I don't want you to."

Her whisper brushed against his skin, and her lips touched his.

Without any hesitation, Tyren lifted her in his arms, carrying her to his bedroom.

Heavy curtains blocked the afternoon sun, creating the perfect semidarkness. Both their clothes piled in a trail of passion leading to the oversized bed, and Tyren finally unleased the desire burning inside him.

Caranna surprised him with an equally blazing want, unafraid to surrender herself to his demanding kisses.

One by one, all the pieces of his soul fell into their place, making him whole again.

"This moment, right now, is the identical reflection of one of those flash visions you had back on Brillum." Tyren regained his wits, drawing Caranna in his arms after they recovered from the sweet and passionate union.

"Yes, it is." Her hand gently glided on the side of his face, fingertips trailing over his scar.

"Would it be safe to assume the rest of them

were just as accurate?" He covered her hand with his, kissing her palm.

"I don't know." She smiled. "Maybe?"

"Then, I would like you to move here." Tyren rolled over, pinning her under his body.

"I already live in your home." Her index finger traced a line along his nose. "Did you have your nose broken?"

Sure, she would've noticed his slightly crocked nose, only visible at a closer examination. The memory of the day it happened, sparked in his mind.

"Yes, I did. The first day in the Academy I had a confrontation."

Her laughter filled the room. "You didn't waste any time, did you?"

"No." He wrapped his arms around her, kissing the laughter off her lips. "I'm serious, Cara. I know you accepted the suite next door, but I want you in here with me."

"Why?" Her chocolatey eyes narrowed with suspicion.

"You mean other than the obvious?" Tyren let his hand slide over her body, under the silk sheet.

"Yes." Her body answered his touch, her back arched and one of her legs wrapped around his.

"It would be easier to make sure you're safe." His

lips kissed a trail on the side of her neck, to her shoulder.

"You do realize that I am perfectly capable of taking care of myself, right?" For each of his kisses she answered with her own, across his chest.

Tyren cupped her face between his hands. "I want you to be the last thing I see before I fall asleep and the first to see when I wake up."

Her lips parted, but no words came out. Just a silent sigh touched his skin like a torch.

"No." Caranna shook her head. "I think you are getting a little ahead of yourself here. Those visions you saw in my mind, may come true tomorrow, or in twenty years from now. Don't rush."

Tyren let himself fall on his back, beside her. He didn't want to pressure her yet having her in his bed felt so right.

"Since you need your training today," an idea crossed his mind, "I propose a game."

"Why do I have the feeling that I won't like it?" Caranna turned on her side, facing him.

"We both go outside, and the first one to disarm the other wins. No energy use." Propped on an elbow, he brushed from her face a couple of rebel strands of hair.

"You're kidding, right?" Her laughter filled his

ears and slipped into his heart. "Why would I accept a challenge I have no chance of winning? You're about twice my size, and I'll be overpowered in no time."

"Cara, you will most probably always be overpowered by your opponents. It is why you will need to get creative."

"Creative?" She sat, tightening the sheet around her small frame.

"You're fast, use it to your advantage. And do you remember what I told you about distraction?" Tyren slid his legs over the edge of the bed.

"Yes, I used it earlier today, on Khaon." She didn't move an inch, but her gaze followed his every movement.

Tyren stood, facing her. "Exactly. You are not helpless in combat. Learn your abilities and use them."

Her head tilted to the side, and an amused smirk danced on her lips. "All right. You're on," she accepted his challenge.

Minutes later, showered and in training clothes, Tyren faced her in the middle of the grassy area between the swimming pool and the large, shaded patio.

With no doubt in his mind that he could disarm

her anytime he wanted, Tyren passed on the first opportunity. Not to mention, he thoroughly enjoyed watching her in action.

Caranna's speed kept him alert, but her slim body, running circles around him, distracted him a few times. Every time she came close to grabbing his sword, he caught her arm, pulling her close for a kiss.

"You're not trying hard enough." He released her, taking a step back. "Again."

Eyes narrowed, she launched her body into his, surprising and knocking him off his feet. On instinct, his arms closed around her, tumbling in the soft grass together.

"What, you didn't see it coming?" Her laughter filled the late afternoon hot and humid air.

Tyren caught her hand only a couple of inches away from his sword. "Well played, but you still don't have my sword." He rolled over, straddling her.

One hand holding both her arms above her head, he lowered on top of her for yet another kiss. His other hand detached her sword from the belt across her hips, laying it in the grass, above her head.

The kiss evolved from sweet and innocent, into deep and passionate, and he released her arms, with his own agenda in mind.

Caranna's small hands slipped under his shirt,

and his roamed over her smooth skin, under the loose tank top she wore.

"Aha." With a sudden move, Caranna rolled him to the side and sat on top of him. "I win." She brought her hand, holding his sword, between them.

A victorious smirk danced on the kiss swollen lips.

"Good try," Tyren nodded toward her sword, still lying in the grass.

She followed his gaze, and the moment she saw her weapon just above the spot where her head rested only seconds ago, her shoulders slumped. "I didn't even notice when you grabbed it."

"That's because you lost your focus." Tyren reattached his sword on his belt, then drew her closer to him.

"I was focused." She shook her head.

"On what?" Tyren couldn't help but smile.

"You." Her arms closed around his waist.

"While I can't say I mind it," he leaned in for another kiss, "I have to remind you that you need to keep your goal in mind. Distraction goes both ways."

He lifted his left hand, holding her strapless bra.

"When did you get that?" She hurried to cover her chest with both her arms.

"When you let your guard down." Tyren rolled

her over again, holding her close. "Never, ever, let your opponent distract you."

Caranna yanked her bra from his hand. "I guess now I have to move in with you."

"Was there any doubt in your mind?" Tyren winked. Something about her made him feel lighter, playful, as if when his soul pieced back together some pieces exchanged places.

"No, I knew I would lose." She lifted her head off the grass, to plant a couple of kisses on his chest.

"Then why did you accept the challenge?" His brows furrowed, confusion slipping in his mind.

"I wanted to make you work for it." Her whisper filled his being with desire, as if she had hit a switch.

Tyren couldn't stop the laughter. "I have the feeling that our lives together won't be boring." His hungry lips took hers in another kiss.

I had no idea she would crash into my life, make a mess of everything, and I'd be enjoying every moment of it.

13

Caranna

Four months later, Caranna rode on the back seat of Tyren's speeder, toward the open-air spaceport.

"I can't wait to go home." She leaned her head on his back, her arms tightening around his waist.

"What? You didn't like Fanaris?" His laughter filled her ears through the comm system.

She'd made a point in telling him every chance she got how much she hated the world of Fanaris. A void planet, where energy users couldn't connect to their power, she felt like she'd been walking around half blind.

"You know how I feel about this world." Caranna closed her eyes, refusing to see more of the depressing landscape.

Not only had Fanaris felt dead, it looked the part, too, with its constant fog, never-ending swamps, and lack of color. For the past four months, she'd never felt dry, or seen the sun.

Gray trees dotted the landscape, their roots disappearing under the murky waters, the limbs covered with an identical coloration hanging moss instead of leaves.

Hell, even the grass is gray in this awful world.

"At least you got pretty good with a blaster." Tyren glanced toward her over a shoulder.

"Not by choice." Caranna reopened her eyes and placed a small kiss on his cheek.

Without her connection to the energies, and the ongoing battle between the federation and coalition troops, she was forced to use a blaster pistol in addition to sharpening her sword and combat skills.

Tyren had always been by her side, they watched each other's backs, and made a great team. Even without the use of energy.

"You should know," Tyren glanced back at her again, "we're not going straight home."

"We're not?" She straightened her spine.

Caranna was looking forward to at least a couple of days of well-deserved, hard-earned rest.

"No. We're making a three-day stop on the way."

"Where?" She peeked over his shoulder at the dirt road ahead, the visibility reduced to about six feet by the ever-present fog.

"Surprise." His smile warmed her from the inside. "Tomorrow is your birthday, and I thought we should celebrate it properly."

Her heart flipped in her chest. Tyren wasn't just her mentor anymore, he'd become the man she loved, the center of her existence.

"Can you at least give me a clue? What if I don't like it?"

She felt in the palms of her hands, his laughter before hearing it.

"I very much doubt that." He pointed to the screen displaying the map. "We should be at the shuttle in twenty minutes or so. If my calculations are correct, we should arrive at our destination some-time tomorrow. It's a six-hour flight in hyperspace."

"Six hours?" She tried to figure out by herself the probable destination of their mini-vacation, but she wasn't familiar with the Outer Fringe.

"C'mon, one clue won't ruin the surprise." Caranna kissed the side of his neck.

"Okay," he seemed to give in to her plea, "sun."

"That's hardly a clue. It can be anywhere other than here." She slapped his shoulder. "A decent hint?"

"Is water better?" Tyren squeezed her thigh, then returned his hand to the controls of the speeder.

"No, it's not."

"Fine." Tyren winked at her. "It will involve a blindfold."

"For me or for you?" Convinced he was joking, she joined in the fun.

"You first." He turned his head toward her. "I might try one later."

She couldn't help but laugh and cuddle closer into his back side.

A loud shot followed by the speeder's sudden veering, as if Tyren lost control of it, sent both of them tumbling in the mud. The mud and puddles offered a somewhat softer landing for the tangled mess of their limbs, yet a sharp pop quickly followed by pain pierced through her left wrist.

Only steps away, the vehicle hit one of the dead looking trees exploding to pieces.

"Are you all right?" He hurried to help her up, despite his stiff left shoulder.

"My hand," she closed her right hand over the painful wrist.

"Let me see." Tyren checked, then lifted his gaze to hers. "It's not broken. But it appears you sprained it."

"Ugh. Is your shoulder all right? Caranna touched his arm.

"I think it popped out of place. Is nothing." Tyren dismissed his injury. "Can you stand?"

"Yes." She gathered her feet under her. "What the hell happened?"

"Stay low." One hand on her waist, he drew his blaster with the other. "Somebody shot our speeder."

"Did you see the direction of the shot?" Caranna made her blaster ready, her gaze sweeping over the gray surroundings. The fog covered everything in mystery.

The enemy could be anywhere.

"No." Tyren scanned the area, then stopped by one of the depressing looking trees. "But whoever it is, can't be far. They needed to see us through the fog."

The sound of a shot filled the air, and the red streak of a charge cut through the milky fog.

"Ty." Caranna threw herself in front of him.

On instinct, Tyren fired back. A loud shriek

followed by a splash, assured her their attacker was at least severely injured, if not dead.

Pain tore through her left shoulder, just below the collarbone. The burn of the charge spread through her body like wildfire. For what felt like a long time, she couldn't draw breath. Caranna lowered her gaze to the wound. Through the torn leather, her skin turned almost black from the burn of the charge, and blood gurgled from the tiny hole.

"Cara." Tyren hugged her to him, easing her onto the muddy ground. "Why would you do that?"

Out of breath, and suddenly weakened, she couldn't articulate any words. She surrendered to his care, trying to hold back the nausea rising in her throat.

"I'm calling for help. Hang on." Tyren opened the cover of his bracer and dialed a frequency.

The surrounding fog appeared to slip inside her mind and body. Moving was almost impossible, as if the shot severed all communication between her brain and the rest of her body.

Tyren's words, his orders, all mixed in a senseless noise, and Caranna closed her eyes.

"Hurry. She's bleeding." His last words somehow found their way into her scrambled mind.

With quick movements, he placed two kovor

patches on her wound—one on top of each other, trying to control the stream of crimson blood.

"Cara, stay with me." He leaned against the tree's thick trunk, holding her in his arms. "Don't you dare die on me. I love you."

She lifted her gaze to his golden eyes.

"I love you, too." The words left her lips with ease.

His gentle kiss on her forehead somehow made her feel better, numbed the excruciating pain for a little while.

"Don't talk." He drew her closer. "Save your strength and stay alive."

"Is he dead?" She grabbed his sleeve.

"I think so. If not, he would've taken another shot at us by now."

Heavy, round drops of rain started to fall over them, and Caranna leaned her head on his good shoulder, making sure she didn't bring him more pain by touching the dislocated one.

"Ty, do you remember when we met," she tried to remain in control of her senses between labored breaths, "you asked me if I would die for you."

"Yes, I remember." One of his hands glided over her hair, pressing her head onto his shoulder.

"Back then, I said I wouldn't." She gathered all

the strength she could and lifted her head, staring at him. "Now I would."

"Cara, I don't want you to die for me." Tyren kissed her lips. "I want you to live with me."

Her pulse accelerated, and with it, the pain scaled up.

"Ty. . ." Her hands clutched the fabric of his robe.

If she was to die, at least she would do so in his arms.

"Shh. The shuttle is almost here."

From somewhere, she couldn't tell direction anymore, the sound of engines sounded closer and closer.

Shivers coursed through her body. The cold rain pelted her skin, and despite Tyren's efforts to keep her calm and breathing, it became harder to keep her eyes open. She let the cold and sudden tiredness win, falling into sweet semi consciousness.

A light rocking motion lulled her, and low whispers entered her mind.

"Hang on Cara. Please stay with me. Don't leave me. Not now. Not ever." Tyren's voice, even if dropped so low she could barely hear it, motivated her to reopen her eyes. One of her flash visions popped in her mind—the perfect replica of the present.

Rain now poured over them and mixed with the tears running on his face. In her wildest dreams she couldn't have imagined the man feared by an entire galaxy, crying.

She had no idea if it had been seconds, minutes, or an eternity since they sat in the mud.

"I love you, Ty." With the last of her strength, she lifted a hand and wiped his tears.

"Then stay with me." The sounds of an engine drew closer, almost covering his words.

Caranna tried to smile, but she wasn't sure she did. Her own body didn't seem to respond to any commands anymore. The hand touching his face turned heavy and fell by her side.

"Cara." Tyren's panic was the last thing she heard.

The cold dissipated, she didn't feel the rain any longer, and nothingness swallowed her.

14

Tyren

AFTER A LAST ROUND of the property, setting everything just the way he wanted it, Tyren took off his shirt and threw it on the floor. To make sure his shoulder had fully healed he drew a wide arc with his left arm. Without any pain or discomfort, he neared the bed.

Caranna stirred under the white sheets, the first movement in the last twelve hours.

"Welcome back, my love." He kissed her temple and lay beside her.

A smile parted her lips before she even opened her eyes. "Ty."

"Happy birthday." He hugged her to him, closing his eyes in relief for a moment.

Yes, she'd been outside any danger for hours, but he couldn't wait to see her back to her usual self.

"You smell so good," she whispered, then placed a kiss on his shoulder. "Umm. . . Where are we?" Caranna tensed, her arms closing around him.

"On our vacation. How are you feeling?"

"Incredibly well rested. Wait, I got shot, didn't I?" Caranna quickly checked her shoulder, now fully healed. "What about your shoulder?"

"Yes, you did. But after the surgery and two hours in a healing tank, you're like new." He gently glided his fingertips over the new skin covering any trace of her earlier wound. "Not even a scar. And my shoulder is fixed, too."

"How long have I been out? I can't remember anything after hearing the shuttle near."

"Twelve hours since you lost consciousness." Tyren propped on an elbow. "Don't you ever do that again, Cara."

"Lose consciousness?" One of her hands slid over his shoulder, stopping in the middle of his chest.

"Risk your life for me." Tyren shook his head. "I have never been so scared in my life. I thought I lost you." He lifted her hand to his lips, kissing it.

"It is what we do, Ty." Cara gathered the sheet around her. "We keep each other alive. How many times did you take a hit for me on that blasted Fanaris?"

"That's my job." Tyren had never kept count. He would've preferred he was injured rather than her.

"Did you find out who it was?"

"No one we know." Tyren stood. "Some mercenary who didn't get to complete his job."

Wrapped in the sheet, Caranna slid her feet over the edge of the bed, then rose.

"What time is it?" She took a step toward the closed curtains.

"Time for you to see where we are." Tyren stopped her, dragging her in the opposite direction, toward the door.

From the first step outside, on the wooden deck, Caranna froze in place. Her gaze shifted from the tray filled with snacks and champagne, to the unusual wooden deck, and then to the breathtaking sunset.

"Ty," she stared in his eyes, "this is the most beautiful place I've ever seen." Arms wrapped around him, she appeared to refocus on the surroundings.

The deck stopped after fifteen or so feet, but a

thick wooden frame continued for another ten feet, along the whole width of the floor. A white net stretched over the frame instead of wooden planks, offering a view to the crystal-clear water underneath.

"This is the sanctuary world of Daraas." Instinctively, he drew her closer. "How about a snack and some champagne? We have dinner reservations for later."

"Okay." She lifted her face to him. "Thank you for bringing me here."

"If you like it, we can extend our stay to a week. Or come back anytime." He helped her walk over the edge of the wooden frame, and onto the sturdy net replacing the floor three to four feet above the water level.

"Is this going to hold us both?" She seemed hesitant to walk over the slightly bouncing net.

"It's guaranteed to hold up to two thousand pounds." Unlike her, he walked on with confidence.

Earlier he covered one end of it with a couple of comforters and threw on a few pillows for additional coziness, after experiencing the hard cords digging onto the bottom of his feet.

One hand over a pocket, Tyren attempted to control his racing heart.

This is crazy. I haven't been this nervous since my first date, as a teenager.

"Look at this sky." Cara tightened the sheet around her body, holding it from flying off in the soft breeze.

On the horizon, the sun glowed in hues of orange against the red sky. The shades of crimson transitioned into golds, deep blues, only to turn purple above them.

Hundreds of indigo clouds hung in the air like tiny pieces of cotton, outlined in bright yellow by the setting sun.

"It is quite a show." He poured champagne in the two flutes, handing her one. "Happy birthday, my love. Make a wish." Tyren kissed her, then wrapped an arm around her shoulders.

"My wish has already come true." Cara smiled, then sipped from her drink. "I am here, with you. What more can I wish for?"

Tyren took her glass and placed it beside his, on the silver tray.

"Let's see if I can help with that." He lowered himself on one knee in front of her.

"What are you doing?" She took a step back.

"Cara," he took out the ring burning a hole in his pocket and held it in front of her. "I love you more than life itself. I want you to be my best friend, my partner, my lover, the mother of our children, my wife, my everything, just as I hope I can be for you."

"Ty. . ." Tears glazed her eyes.

"You know me better than anyone else in the world. I lay at your feet everything I am—my sword, my heart, my love for you. Would you marry me?" He finally asked the question filling his mind for months.

"Yes." Her voice trembled, and Cara kneeled in front of him. "A million times yes." Tiny tears left her eyes, running on her face.

Tyren slipped the ring on her finger, then kissed her. The sunset, the soft breeze, the sound of low waves, all melted away.

She is my everything, my entire world.

In each other's arms, Tyren rolled her onto the puffy comforters, getting lost in his love for the only woman who had ever conquered his heart.

"I wish I could stop time." He slowly readjusted to reality after love and passion had consumed his body and soul.

"Wouldn't it be a bliss if this moment could last forever?" Cara lay her head on his shoulder.

"It is up to us to always feel this way." Tyren let

the energies gathered inside him spread out, close around both of them like a cocoon.

"Just when I thought I couldn't love you more, you proved me wrong." She stretched in his arms, her lips touching his.

"I love you, too. I can't even imagine my life without you." He kissed her back, holding her close. "How soon do you think we can have a ceremony?"

"Umm. . ." She hesitated, as if searching for the right words. "I'd like to wait until after I pass my trials."

"What? That's six months from now." Tyren stacked a couple more pillows under his head.

"I know." She lowered her gaze for a moment, then looked him in his eyes. "Where I'm coming from, the first, most basic way a woman honors her husband is by taking his name."

"Lady Caranna Tebbet," he murmured. "It sounds good."

"It does, and I can't wait to change my name," Cara smiled. "But I want to honor my family, too. I'd like to be registered in the Academy's archives as Dark Lady Caranna Baro. Just once, I want to hear someone calling me that." A shy smile stretched her lips.

How can I say no to her? I can't. Period.

"All right. I understand and respect that." He drew her back in his arms. "But your training just went up another notch."

"Why?" Her eyes rounded in surprise and confusion.

"Because I have to make sure you pass those trials. I'm not going to wait another year for a second attempt."

Her wholehearted laughter filled his ears and his heart.

Stars I want to hear her laugh like this every day. She makes me happy.

"I think I'll pass those trials with flying colors. After all, I have the best mentor." She molded her body against him. "You have already taught me so much."

"There are still a few thinks I need to teach you." Tyren winked, kissing her again. He couldn't help himself.

"Like what?" Mischievousness reflected in her chocolatey eyes, and a playful tone sent his blood in a rush.

"Remember I told you yesterday that our vacation would involve a blindfold?" His hands slipped under the sheet covering them, unable to control his urge to touch her. "Initially I intended to use it on our arrival here, so you wouldn't see this view until the right moment."

"And that changed?" One of her hands glided on his chest, toward his abdomen.

"You were still sedated when we got here, so I didn't need it. But it would be a shame to have it and not put it to beneficial use. Maybe tonight, after dinner."

For a second time her laughter that he loved so much, filled the air. "That would be a shame indeed."

Tyren pulled the sheet over both of them, then pinned her body under his. The need to feel her close overrode everything else.

15

Caranna

AFTER FOUR MONTHS on the battlefields of Fanaris, and a week vacation on Daraas, Caranna stepped out on the covered patio in Tyren's home on Simran.

My home now, too. She coiled her arms around his waist.

"Thank you so much for surprising me with bringing Fira here." Caranna lifted on her toes and planted a kiss on his cheek.

"I figured you would feel better if you had her here with us." He drew her closer.

"How did you even find her?" Caranna looked in

his golden eyes, a never-ending source of strength, love, and a peaceful yet exciting feeling.

"It wasn't that hard." Tyren kissed to top of her head. "You said she stayed in your great grandmother's home." He walked to one of the outdoor couches.

"You are spoiling me." Caranna sat beside him.

"You are making me happy." He countered, his arms tightening around her frame, his lips demanding her full attention.

Raised voices from inside the house interrupted their blissful moment.

"What is going on?" She withdrew from his arms.

Before Tyren had a chance to answer, the doors to the living room opened wide, and his mother marched in.

"Mother." His brows furrowed.

"I'm sorry, My Lord." One of the servants followed her. "I tried to stop her."

"It is all right." Tyren waved a dismissive hand toward the frightened servant, then refocused on his mother. "You should have let me know you were coming, Mother. Or knocked."

"We need to talk." She stopped in the middle of the spacious patio. "Alone."

The look in his mother's eyes when she saw her,

made Caranna feel like an insect, an intruder. Her first impulse was to leave, but Tyren's hand closed over hers, holding her in place.

"Cara and I don't have secrets. Whatever you have to say to me, she can hear it, too." Tyren gestured to the couch across from the coffee table.

Lady Vione lifted her chin with defiance. "Very well." Shoulders stiff and spine straight, she sat on the edge of the couch. "I have done a little research." She placed a data pad on the table, beside the tray filled with refreshments and snacks.

"What kind of research?" Tyren grabbed the device, activating it.

Cara drew closer to him, staring at the pictures of her family displayed on the flat screen.

"You ran a background check on me?" Golden sparks gathered around her hands, ready to ignite.

Tyren's mother glanced at her for a moment, disgust filling her eyes, only to return her attention to her son. "Did you know she's marked? Did she tell you?"

"What are you talking about?" He lifted his gaze from the pictures of her, and her family, to his mother. "And who gave you permission to dig in Cara's life?"

"I hired an agent." Lady Vione Tebbet leaned

forward. "And I'm glad I did." She pointed an index finger at the data pad. Her gloves matched the color of her pencil skirt in the exact same shade of cream. "All her family is marked." Her tone scaled up.

"Marked?" Tyren powered off the data pad and placed it back on the table in front of his mother.

"You can't tell me you didn't notice the silver hair she's hiding now." Lady Vione grabbed the device and shoved it in her purse.

"So? I knew she had silver hair since the first time I met her over six years ago." Tyren seemed confused.

"That's the mark of someone who will bring destruction." A hint of victory echoed in his mother's voice.

Caranna's heart stopped in her chest. Her great grandmother told her once that their family was destined for greatness. How was it possible for two opinions to be so different?

"Mother, I don't believe in your superstitions." He grabbed one of the glasses filled with fruit juice. "Would you like a drink?" Tyren offered to pour a glass for his mother.

"I'm not here for pleasantries. You need to get rid of her."

Get rid of me? What am I, some used-up useless

piece of trash? Caranna fought the anger expanding in her body and filling her eyes with tears.

To her side, crimson clouds gathered around Tyren, and the glass in his hand shattered. Glass shards and fruit juice splashed all around him.

"Cara and I love each other, and this week we've become engaged." The muscles in his square jaw twitched. "We will get married the day after she passes her Lordship trials in a few months."

"No." His mother's eyes widened with terror. "You can't bring someone like her," she gestured toward Caranna, "in our family. Her children, their children, and so on, will all have the mark." Her words sounded like a sentence. "I forbid it."

"You have no right to tell me how to live my life." Tyren stood, both his hands closed in fists by his sides.

Caranna picked up on the energies swirling around them, the tension filling his body, and the hurt stabbing his heart.

"I am your mother." Lady Vione confronted her son.

"No. You brought me into this world. The nannies, servants and slaves who cared for me were more mothers to me than you will ever be." Tyren leaned a couple of inches over the low table. "You were too busy hating me for ruining your waistline."

"You're forgetting all the parties I took you to? All the people you've met?" Green sparks flickered in her emerald eyes.

"You only showed me off to your narrow-minded friends." Tyren straightened. "If only once you would've taken the time to play with me, or just talk. But you were too busy going to parties and entertaining guests."

"Someone had to keep our family's name in all the right places." Defiance rose in waves from his mother's perfect frame. "Your useless father did nothing for us."

"Don't you dare taint my father's name and memory. He's been one of the most respected Dark Lords our order has ever had." Tyren's anger made the deep red clouds charge with energy, as if a storm was about to hit. "He taught me everything I know."

"Right, your precious order." His mother spat. "He neglected his family for it."

"No mother, he didn't. You pushed him away with your behavior." Tyren's eyes flickered, as if lightning struck his gold irises. "Obviously, the word *family* has different meanings for us." He let out a sigh.

"Tyren, listen to me. She is going to destroy you." For a second time, his mother pointed toward Caranna.

This time she stood by his side. "You don't even know me. How can you accuse me like this?" Caranna had a hard time controlling her anger. If the other woman wasn't Tyren's mother she would've been dead, struck where she stood. "I love Tyren, and I would die rather than hurt him in any way."

"I wasn't talking to you." Lady Vione threw her an arrogant glance.

"Mother, if you want to be welcomed in our home, you will do well to learn respect for the woman I love." Tyren stepped forward. "If you can't accept Cara, we have nothing more to discuss."

"I can't believe you are taking her side." His mother's tone scaled up, and her chin jutted forward. "She carries a bad seed, and your children, future generations will too."

"Do not make me choose, Mother. You won't like my choice." Tyren wrapped an arm around Caranna's waist, making it clear where his loyalty was. "Cara is my future. We'll build our own family. It is up to you if you want to be a part of it or not."

Lady Vione Tebbet squared her shoulders. "I see I'm not welcome anymore in my son's home." She took a step toward the door. "Mark my words," she stopped and stared at Tyren, "she will bring you a great deal of suffering."

Like an actor on stage, his mother started to the door, her high heels clicking on the stone floor, each movement exaggerated to make a point.

"Ty." Caranna waited until his mother crossed the living room and exited. "I don't want to cause a rift between you and your mother."

"You are not." He hugged her to him. "She did many years ago."

She leaned her head on his chest, finding her calm in his arms. The tension in his body slowly dissipated.

"I'm really sorry, Cara." Guilt seemed to have replaced his earlier anger.

"What if she's right?" Caranna lifted her gaze to his. "Maybe there is something about me, the reason why everyone had always rejected me." Worry wrapped around her heart.

"Don't tell me you believe in her superstitions. They're nothing more than excuses. She's only looking for reasons to reject you because you're not *nobility*." Tyren cupped her face between his hands. A few drops of blood trickled from a cut across his palm.

"You cut yourself." She covered his hand with hers. "I'll get you a kovor patch." Caranna tried to walk away from him, but his hold on her tightened.

"Cara, I love you. Nothing in this world would ever change that." His lips crashed over hers, his kiss making her forget about the cut on his hand, and the second disastrous meeting with his mother.

"I love you, too."

16

Tyren

THE DAY OF THE TRIALS, Tyren stood with the other mentors watching their apprentices fighting their way through each challenge.

In the morning, Caranna had passed the written tests. She would've done it with a perfect score if not for misspelling the name of one of the members of the Dark Circle. An involuntary smile tugged at the corner of his mouth, remembering how she renamed Lord Gowon to Lord Goon.

Fitting, he mused. *He's always in charge with the heavy lifting in their little clique.*

"My Lord." A voice from behind forced him to tear his gaze from the screen showing Caranna fighting another group of beasts in the catacombs under the ancient City of the Dead.

"Yes?" He turned to see who disturbed him at such an inappropriate time. "Oh." His mood suddenly improved when he recognized the jeweler that he'd trusted with a gift for Caranna.

"It's ready." The other man handed him a tiny satchel.

"Not a moment too soon." Tyren opened the pouch, letting the pendant slid onto his open palm. "I was starting to worry I wouldn't have a gift for my bride, tomorrow."

"My apologies, My Lord." The man bowed. "It's been close to impossible to put my hands on all this Terudium."

Tyren had insisted the jewelry be made from the most resilient metal in existence, the only one that could withstand almost any kind of damage. For some reason, he liked the idea of the jewelry lasting as long as his love for Cara—for an eternity. He turned the pendant between his fingers, the initials CT bringing another smile to his lips.

"It is perfect." Tyren placed the chain and

pendant back in its satchel. "I trust the credits had been transferred to your account already?"

"Yes, My Lord. Thank you." The jeweler bowed again. "It's been an honor and a pleasure working for you. This is one of my favorite pieces I've ever made. I hope your bride will love it, too."

"I'm sure she will." Tyren slipped the pouch in the pocket inside his robe, just above his heart.

The jeweler nodded, then left, and Tyren refocused on the screen showing Caranna.

She'd just finished another challenge and stopped to recover energy and accelerate her regeneration rate. During the trials, the contestants weren't allowed to use healing patches.

A few scratches marked her arms, and it appeared one of the beasts managed to claw Caranna's thigh. Three parallel lines ran deep on her leg, blood seeping through the ripped leather.

Take your time, my love. The hardest part is yet to come.

Tyren glanced toward the other screens showing all contenders. Of the twelve that started over an hour ago, only six were left to claim their titles.

By the exit from the catacombs, two bodies lay on the ground, covered with black sheets. One of them belonged to Khaon. A third contestant was in the healers' care, unconscious. The other three forfeit their trials already, before even reaching the half-way mark.

Caranna advanced through the dark corridor and into the next room. The door closed behind her, and electromagnetic fields activated, cutting her connection with the energies.

Shoulders tensed, Tyren leaned closer to the screen. From one of the dark corners, instead of a droid, a silhouette drew toward the middle until he recognized the man—Major Marek.

"What in the stars?" He straightened, a cold shiver coursing along his spine. "This is not part of the trials. How did he get in there?" Tyren attracted the attention of everyone around.

"Afraid your apprentice can't defeat a non-user?" The sarcasm in Dark Lord Brode's words echoed over the general murmurs of the other mentors. "Would you like to pull her out?"

All mentors had the option to interrupt their apprentices' trials, forfeit them.

"She was supposed to face a droid in there." Fists closed, Tyren took in a deep breath in an effort to control his anger. "Someone interfered with the course." He pointed an accusatory finger at the screen.

The smirk on Lord Brode's face assured him he wasn't a stranger to the situation. He didn't seem affected by the loss of his apprentice.

I wouldn't be surprised if he's responsible for it.

"The trials are meant to test the limits of the contestants, not coddle them." Dark Lord Dovor joined in, his apprentice one step behind him.

"Easy to say when your boy didn't have the guts to go in." Tyren refocused on the screen, knowing now that Caranna's challenge was a set-up orchestrated by his nemeses.

She didn't appear intimidated, and he turned up the volume. If need be, he would forfeit her trials, but he had faith in her abilities, and her training.

"Major Marek." Her voice came through calm and collected. "This is a surprise." A wide smile parted her lips.

"You won't think so in a minute." Major Marek leveled a blaster pistol in her direction.

"Why would you want to kill me?" She took a small step closer to the major. "I thought we were friends. By the way, I still owe you a dinner."

"You have ruined my plans enough." Marek's

voice hardened, but he seemed to be smart enough to retreat in front of her.

"What are you talking about?" Caranna crossed her arms over her chest with a relaxed attitude. "What plans?"

"You interfered on Brillum." Marek's voice scaled up an octave. "That was such a good set-up. If it wasn't for you, Lord Tebbet would've died that day."

"Hey, I needed a mentor. If you told me what you were up to, I would've looked for someone else to get me where I am now." Caranna shifted her weight from one leg to the other but added a small step forward to the movement.

Tyren recognized one of her tactics—keep him talking and distracted until she was close enough to initiate a surprise attack.

"What about Fanaris? You almost died for him. I planned all that so carefully." Frustration rose in the major's voice. "You are in love with him, engaged to get married tomorrow."

"Ha." Caranna's amusement stabbed Tyren's heart. "That proves that you don't know much about women." She uncrossed her arms taking another step forward.

"What do you mean?"

"I'm only using him to get my title, silly." Her voice turned seductive with a little too much ease for Tyren's liking. "Why do you think I insisted we get married *after* I pass my trials?"

Major Marek appeared hesitant, the blaster pistol in his hand lowered a few inches. "You're messing with me."

"Why would I? You have to admit that there was something between us ever since we met, back on Brillum." She ached a brow. "Don't tell me I was wrong to believe so."

"N . . . No, but. . . How do I know that you're not just trying to get out of getting killed?" The major aimed his pistol again.

"How about we unite efforts? I'll help you kill him after I finish my trials." Caranna's sweet voice inflicted pain in Tyren's heart.

Stars, please let this be just a tactic and not true.

"You would do that?" For a second time the major lowered his weapon.

"Of course. I don't care about him, and never intended to marry him." She waved a dismissive hand. "Or do you need approval from whomever you work for?"

She's trying to get more information.

Tyren followed her subtle movement toward the

other man. The way she swayed her hips, guaranteed to attract any man's attention, brough hope back into his heart.

"Why do you think I'm working for someone?" Marek retreated another step.

"Because I'm not stupid." Caranna's laughter filled the vast underground room, echoing against the crude walls. "Who is it? Those three clowns in the Dark Circle?" She winked. "Lord Brode, Lord Dovor, and Lord Gowon had made their dislike known every chance they got."

Tyren had to bite the inside of his cheek to hold back a chuckle. To his side, anger and revolt rose from the three dark lords in discussion.

"How did you know?" Major Marek's eyes widened to the point where they were ready to pop out of their sockets.

"Let's call it feminine intuition." One more step, and Caranna placed a hand on the major's shoulder. "What do you say? Are we allies, or enemies?"

Before the man had a chance to answer, she rushed the blade of her sword in his abdomen, twisting it for good measures. Hunched over, the major collapsed to his knees, and Caranna pulled back her sword. Blood gurgled from his body, and life drained from his eyes. Another second later, he lay on the dirt floor.

That's my girl.

"And now I have the proof that you three have been behind at least two assassination attempts." Tyren faced the other dark lords.

"That doesn't count as proof." With one trembling index finger pointed to the screen, Dark Lord Dovor was the first to object.

"Actually, it does." Lord Raz Harett appeared out of nowhere by Tyren's side. "According to our laws, all three of you are dismissed from your positions with the Dark Circle."

"We have the right to contest what that man said." Dark Lord Brode joined his ally.

"The declaration of a dying man is undeniable." Raz Harett stood his ground.

"He wasn't dying when he involved us." Lord Gowon tried his luck.

"Trust me, he was dying since he walked in there." Tyren pointed to the screen showing Caranna limping out of the room.

Lord Raz Harett signaled a group of guards to approach. With the soldiers, the sixth member of the Dark Circle, Lord Kerron, approached.

"As the mediator of our council I am here to

relieve you from duty." Dark Lord Kerron's voice attracted more attention to the scene. "Escort them to the holding cells where they'll wait for their trials." He turned toward the guards.

"Your apprentice is brilliant." Lord Harett faced Tyren. The guards dragged the other three dark lords away in protest. "You have trained her well, my friend."

Maybe too well. For a moment even I believed her.

"Thank you. She was the perfect apprentice." Tyren refocused on the screen.

Caranna made it through the last two challenges, and finally stepped out of the catacombs in the red light of the sunset.

Out of breath, hands propped on her knees, she doubled over.

"Cara." Tyren ran to her.

Four officials waited and stopped him before he reached her. She had to walk by herself to the committee's podium and receive her title.

Barely touching the ground with her injured leg, Caranna mostly hopped her way to the officials.

"Congratulations for passing your trials." One of them spoke with a solemn voice. "From today forward, you will be known as Dark Lady Caranna Baro."

Pride filled Tyren's heart.

"If you wouldn't mind signing here, My Lady." Another one of the officials handed her a data pad. "It's for the order's archives."

With a trembling hand and eyes swimming in tears, she signed her name and returned the flat device, receiving in exchange her golden sash.

Every single dark lord, or lady, received a sash in the color of their choice, with the letters *DL* embroidered on top of the order's insignia. It was the proof of their title, usually displayed in their offices.

"Cara." Tyren finally hurried to her side. "Congratulations, my love. You did it." He lifted her in his arms.

"Yes, I did." A faint smile parted her lips through exhaustion and pain.

"We need a healer." He yelled toward the improvised shade-tents lined only steps away.

"Over here." He recognized the same medic from the Citadel who had healed Cara before.

"What about the others?" She glanced back, to exit from catacombs.

"Khaon is one of those," he nodded in the direction of the bodies covered with black sheets. "Vitez withdrew the last moment, and Pollex is unconscious somewhere under those tents."

"How many others finished?" She seemed somewhat relieved.

"Three, and you're the only woman. There are only two left in, if they make it out." Tyren couldn't stop himself from kissing her forehead. "I'm so proud of you."

As soon as he placed her on the hard mattress, noise coming from one of the transporters, attracted his attention. Cuffed, the three dark lords refused to go quietly.

Despite the heavy, energy disrupting cuffs, Lord Dovor grabbed one of the soldier's blasters, firing one shot in Tyren's direction.

The charge hit his chest, above his heart, knocking all air out of his lungs and sending him to the ground.

"Ty." Caranna's scream reached his ears through the general commotion.

Pain spread through his body, and for a few moments, he couldn't breathe. Two healers hurried to his side.

A few steps away, the guards threw the rebel Dark Lord Dovor in the back of the armored transporter, locking the door.

"I'm all right." He tried to stand, but his legs refused to cooperate, and he fell to his knees.

The two healers helped him to the mattress beside Caranna's. His chest felt like it had collapsed, but he wasn't bleeding. Through the hole in his robe's fabric, he noticed the satchel holding her pendant. Reduced to shreds, the velvety pouch reveled the reason for which he was still alive after being shot.

The Terudium pendant had stopped the charge from punching a hole in his heart, but the impact had left him bruised.

"Are you wearing your armor?" Caranna leaned forward over the edge of the mattress. Worry reflected in her eyes.

"No." Tyren shook head. "Even better." He closed his fist, holding her pendant.

"What do you mean?" She swatted away one of the nurses trying to get her to lay down.

"Your wedding gift saved my life." He opened his fist, showing her the black pendant. "It's made of Terudium, and it got delivered to me two hours ago."

"It's beautiful." Caranna wiped a couple of tears.

"Look at us." Tyren lay on his back, pushed by one of the healers. "Both injured the day before our wedding."

Caranna slipped her hand in his, and finally let the nurse attend to the scratches on her arms.

"But alive." She whispered, turning her gaze to him. "And together."

Tyren squeezed her hand. "Together."

17

Caranna

THE DAY OF HER WEDDING, Caranna woke cuddled on Tyren's side. Even asleep, his massive body offered her comfort and safety.

I love you, Ty. Her gaze lifted to his angular face. *I love you with all my heart and soul, with everything I am.*

She gently placed a hand on his chest, above his heart, where he got shot the previous day. The bruise had completely disappeared after the healers had done their job. An involuntary smile stretched her lips.

"I take it you like what you see?" His hoarse voice made her chuckle.

"Maybe." Caranna kissed his shoulder.

"Are you ready for today?" Tyren faced her, his gold eyes reflecting all the love she'd dreamed to experience one day. "Ready to vow yourself to me in front of the eternal fire?"

"I've never been more ready for anything in my life."

Tyren's kiss quickly transported her into the realm where nothing else existed other than the two of them.

Just like on Brillum, almost a year ago, a succession of rapid images flashed in her mind. She tried to hang on to them, to see as many details as possible. Now she knew they would come true sooner or later.

The first image, the two of them fighting side by side, filled her with pride. A Dark Lady now, Caranna's confidence in her abilities had scaled up, the same as her love for the man who made it all possible.

A picture-perfect image of the two of them and a baby followed. Unlike before, Caranna felt the happiness the vision revealed.

The next image, Tyren carrying on his shoulders a little boy looking just like him, with the same golden eyes and dark hair, filled her heart with so much love, she expected it to blow to pieces.

More flashes gave her a glimpse of her future life with Tyren—their love, fights, sweet moments with their son, even his mother would be a part of their family.

The last image lingered in her mind the longest. Tyren crying and holding her lifeless body. His pain hurt her and threw her back to reality.

"Did you see them?" She lifted her gaze to Tyren's.

A smile, half happy-half sad, persisted on his lips. "I did. It looks like we'll have a life full of happiness."

"Except for the end." She hid her face in his shoulder.

Tyren's arms wrapped around her, his love enveloped both of them like a soft, old blanket.

"Nobody is looking forward to the end. Don't let it ruin the journey there." He lifted her face to him, his lips touching hers again.

"We're going to have a son." She forced a smile.

"Yes, we will." He hugged her closer. "About that last image," Tyren hesitated, shadows darkening his eyes. "If it turns out to be accurate, and you will die before me, I want you to know I'll follow you soon."

"What?" Caranna pulled back. "You're joking, right?"

"No." He shook his head. "I can't and don't want to live without you." His arms tightened around her.

"Don't tell me you're going to take your own life." The thought alone terrified her, her heart beats accelerating.

"I won't." Tyren rested his chin on top of her head. "But I will go on the first active battlefield and let some worthy coalition warrior take that glory."

Tears filled her eyes, and Caranna coiled her arms around his waist, her hands grabbing onto his back.

"What about our son? He'll need you." She lost the fight with her own tears.

"I'll make sure he'll be well-looked after." A sigh left his lips. "The moment you die, my soul will too. I'd be just an empty shell, and that won't help our son."

"Ty," Caranna sobbed in his arms. "I wish for that vision to never come true."

No matter what the future holds for us, we still have the present, and the journey we will take together.

"You realize, that once you vow yourself to me, I'll become the last man in your life, right?" His hot breath warmed the top of her head. "No other man will ever touch you and live. I will kill him."

Caranna wiped the traces left by tears and tilted her head back, looking in the gold eyes which fascinated her.

"Trust me, if anyone else ever tries to touch me, he won't live long enough for you to kill him. I will." She kissed Tyren.

"I love you so much, Cara."

"I love you, too."

The morning sun filtered through the heavy curtains, announcing the beginning of the happiest day in her life. She refused to think any longer about the end, preferring to focus on the present.

One stray ray of light hit her pendant on the night table by Tyren's side.

"Am I going to wear that for the ceremony?" She nodded toward the highly polished piece of sparkling jewelry.

Tyren followed her gaze and grabbed the ends of the chain.

"I don't know." He winked. "You would only become Caranna Tebbet after the ceremony."

The playfulness dancing in his eyes excited her, made her feel she could do anything as long as he was by her side.

"I think I was born to become Caranna Tebbet." She joined in his game, reaching for the pendant.

"In that case," Tyren kissed her, then placed the pendant around her neck.

The tiny sound of the clasp locking in place had something final to it.

"I'll never take it off." She covered it with an open palm.

"I should take it to the jeweler and have it fixed. There is a dent on the bottom of the *T*." He pointed to the two cursive letters twined together.

"No." Caranna wrapped her body around his. "It's perfect the way it is. This pendant has a history all its own. It saved your life."

Tyren rolled her over in the oversized bed, trapping her under him. "We both know that. But do you want to wear it with that imperfection?"

Caranna nodded. "We are not perfect either. That's the beauty of it all. It's our imperfections that make us who we are." One hand slipped into his hair at the back of his head and drew him closer. "And I love every one of yours."

"I thought a while back you said I was perfect." His laughter filled the room and her heart.

"I said you are perfect for me." She couldn't hold back a chuckle.

"I can live with that." Tyren's kiss numbed her mind. "And today, we are starting our lives together, as husband and wife."

"Yes, our future begins today." Her pulse accelerated.

One lonely thought passed through her mind.

If I'm starting a new life with Ty—a new future, then the dread day when I die and leave him behind will grow closer and closer.

Caranna pushed the idea to the back of her mind.

That day is not here yet. Today is. And tomorrow will follow.

THE END

A FAMILY LEGACY BOOK 2

Want updated information on new releases?
Click HERE to sign up for the Newsletter.

The greatest power one can possess doesn't come from light or darkness, but from a place of love.

When Charisse and Draxen meet shortly after the peace proclamation in the galaxy, they discover the fighting is far from done. In search of answers, they unite efforts against fate, risking their lives for each other.

The most known White Templar healer in the galaxy, Charisse Tarren, always felt a piece was missing in her life—her identity. Raised as an orphan by the templars, she lets a vision lure her in with the promise of an important discovery. But what will she find at the end of the rocky road?

Lord Draxen Harett, a member of the Dark Circle, is the one initiating the first peace treaty in the galaxy after hundreds of years of war. His parents' spirits appear before him, sending him to a forgotten world, where he must make a moment's decision—one which could influence the future of the entire galaxy.

Brought together by unexpected circumstances, and overtaken by their feelings for each other, Charisse and Draxen will have to unite their efforts and fight once again. Will they discover their purpose before one of them dies, or will fate defeat them?

**This is a sweet, closed door romance for ages 14+.

1

Charisse

THE SPEEDER SLOWED despite her foot pressing on the acceleration.

What in the stars? Charisse tapped the screen with an open palm. The display turned blank and useless.

"Great." After a few more yards, the vehicle came to a complete stop. "Now I'm stuck in the wilderness with a malfunctioning speeder and no map." Charisse dismounted with a sigh. "What was I thinking?" She opened the cover of her bracer.

A bright message blinked on the small screen: *No service.*

"How can this be? I can make calls all across the galaxy, in space, but not here?" Charisse closed the bracer, annoyed everything now seemed to work against her.

The winding, black dirt road cut through the forested area like a huge serpent. Ruesha, the remote world, considered savage and underdeveloped, was home to some of the most breathtaking views. Why did her speeder have to break down in a wooded area, where visibility was reduced to as far as the next tree?

Where's Kalina when I need her? She would've kicked the speeder until she made it run again.

A slight smile tugged at the corners of her lips. Her best friend—her only friend—had retired from the smuggler-spy lifestyle after the peace declaration a few months ago.

Charisse scanned her surroundings. Old trees, with trunks as thick as a house reached toward the orange sky. Branches covered in long, soft needles, formed a lacy canopy high above the road.

Why in the stars did I listen to the voice telling me to come here?

The nonstop chatter had plagued her for two weeks, but now, it was completely gone.

Hmm. Strange how it went silent the moment I landed.

She wouldn't be on Ruesha if not for the vision set on a continual loop in her dreams.

In her vision, a woman smiled at her, despite the tears running down her face. Dark, short hair framed a delicate face brightened by sparkling chocolate-colored eyes—same as hers.

Charisse sensed the energy connection with the woman holding her—her mother.

She'd searched the White Templar's database, but she couldn't find anyone resembling the woman from her vision. An energy user, no doubt, her mother must've hidden her identity. Many templars took celibacy oaths, to advance in the ranks higher, faster. Perhaps her mother had taken one, too.

But was a career more important than a newborn baby? Had she been nothing more than an inconvenience in her parents' lives?

The only thing she had left from her mother, was a black pendant with two initials, *CT*. She always carried it with her in a pouch, hidden in one of the secret compartments inside her boots. When templars found her, twenty-six-years ago, she had an identity card, her name written on it—Charisse

Tarren. Only her parents' names were both replaced by one word: unknown.

I hope I find my mother, even if only to ask if it was worth abandoning me. Charisse fought a tinge of anger.

Lately, her emotions had become harder and harder to control. A growing darkness hidden deep inside her seemed to have awakened.

The air moved around, and fluctuations in the energies, assured her people were nearby.

From behind lush bushes, a dozen men clad in maroon-armored dress, came into view. Rifles, blaster pistols and portable cannons pointed toward her.

This can't be a coincidence. They must've used some jamming signal to disable my speeder and my bracer.

"Surrender, Templar." A cold and unforgiving voice spoke from behind a closed helmet. The slight accent on the word *templar*, carried a hint of disgust.

Frustration against the useless speeder and the lack of communications, quickly morphed into a cold calm. Her training as a templar always kicked in when she needed it to.

"Who are you?" Charisse brought both hands before her, one arched above the other, as if holding an invisible ball between them.

Most White Templars meditated and prepared for a fight by pressing their palms together in front of their chest, as if praying. Charisse had found her distinct technique as a child.

The energy flowed through her, warm and calming. Each particle charged with a golden glow, gathering between her hands into a small spark.

"We have orders to take you to our Master, preferably alive. Don't try resisting, or we will be forced to kill you."

The whirring of blasters and rifles echoed in the silent forest.

"Who is your Master?" Charisse took a few steps back to avoid being surrounded by a dozen men, leaving herself an escape route.

The death threat didn't faze her. Growing up, she'd learned that death was a natural part of life, a new beginning for her soul into the energy realm. But she wanted to make it count—die for a good reason.

In normal conditions, she wouldn't have been alone. Her crew would've closed into a protective circle around her.

"You will find out when we take you to him." The same threatening voice, belonging to one of the attackers, echoed in her mind and mixed with the loud drumming of her pulse.

The unusual maroon armor the men wore assured her they didn't belong to any of the groups of rebels she'd encountered in the past. Sturdy leather tunics, with long flaps on the sides, made a distinct warning sound with each of their movements.

"I'm not going anywhere with you." Charisse focused, locking all her emotions away, and allowing the energy to fill her being. The spark of gold between her hands expanded, turning silver. "If your Master wants to talk to me, he can come here."

"Get her." The one who appeared to be the leader of the group yelled to his soldiers, then took a step forward.

The men's heavy armored boots sent vibrations into the forest floor with each step taken.

"Preferably alive. Tolko." He signaled toward one man who appeared to be the strongest in the group.

The named man, Tolko, pointed a portable launcher at her, pressing the trigger.

From experience, Charisse knew how heavy his weapon was. She tried once to lift one off the ground, but she couldn't even move it.

A luminous net meant to capture and cut her

connection with the energies unfolded in the air like a tentacled monster.

Oh no, you won't capture me.

Determined to stand her ground, even without her crew, Charisse opened her arms. She released some of the stored energy, enclosing herself in a protective shield—the strongest in her arsenal.

The net traveled through the air and hit the shield a fraction of a second too late, falling at her feet on the grassy ground.

"Great. She's now shielded." Frustration echoed in the voice of the group's leader. "We can't touch her for three minutes." He pointed a rifle toward her.

Only three minutes? I should be insulted. A tiny smirk tugged at the corners of her lips.

"This is one mission you will fail." Charisse moved her hands in a circular motion, gathering more energy. Empowerment coursed through her veins, filling her with hope. A sphere took shape between her palms, and she pushed it forward.

The ball of silver light cut through her shield, expanded and then exploded in a rain of luminescent icicles, knocking the men off their feet. The sparkling miniature blades covered the area, causing a ground quake, making it impossible for her attackers to regain their footing.

The basic defensive technique for all healers, only affected the enemy. She, and in the past her allies, only felt slight vibrations, offering them an edge in a fight with the partially immobilized attackers.

I was supposed to find answers, not a fight. The voice promised it would reunite me with my mother and solve the mystery of the darkness that shouldn't be in me.

Charisse scanned her surroundings again.

She straightened, relaxing her shoulders. Without her crew, she needed to preserve her energy. Yes, even one of the most powerful healers in the galaxy could run out of energy, not to mention her lack of attack techniques.

Charisse weighed her chances versus the dozen men before her. For the moment, they were all helpless, thanks to the quake, but the cost was too great—it had drained her energy ten times more than if she had shielded and healed her allies.

Inhaling, she closed her eyes and brought her hands together, focusing on inner peace. Meditation was her road to serenity. The less she allowed herself to feel any emotion, the more power gathered inside her.

The chaos around the men struggling to stand—

only to be thrown to the ground again—quieted in her mind.

Ever since she'd been a child, Charisse learned how to block her emotions. Fear was the easiest one for her to lock away, and years of combat helped her master it.

From deep inside her, darkness called, tempted her, but she resisted. Anger had become her weakness recently, the hardest one to control. How did she get herself into such a mess?

A White Templar never gives in to the darkness. The mantra she'd been forced to recite too often, helped her regain control of her emotions.

All the energy spent in shielding herself and creating the quake, replenished itself, and it now hummed through her body. She exhaled, calm and in control, surrendering to the inner peace.

A stir in the air sent strong, distracting pulsations, as if another energy user was nearby, and it yanked her out of meditation. She needed to focus. Slowly, she reopened her eyes to find the group of fighters rising back to their feet.

Spears of light pierced through the laced canopy above her head, hitting their weapons—a reminder that death didn't always came from the darkness. Sometimes, it came from the shiniest places.

This was a trap. The truth hit her mind with clarity, like a derailed freighter. *I need to buy more time, find a way out of this mess I got myself into.*

But if the voice who compelled her to come to Ruesha in the first place was behind the attack, why did it go silent? It could've simply directed her to him.

Are the attackers working for the man behind the voice, or someone else? And if so, who?

Charisse drew more energy, gathering it around herself and into a shimmering, protective shield.

The light vibrations in the ground lessened, and she focused on her adversaries.

Quickly, she formed another ball between her hands and pushed it forward, sending another wave of silvery icicles and quakes.

"Damn it. Not again." One of the attackers tried to remain on his feet, propping his weapon on the forest floor for stability. A vain attempt, he collapsed, joining the others.

She had to do everything in her power to keep the enemy at bay. Surrender was out of the question.

I'll die before letting the voice fool me again.

2

Draxen

"Wait for me at the ship." Draxen mounted on his black speeder. "I'll take one more ride around this backward world, then we're out of here."

"Yes, My Lord." His assistant, Tosek, stacked the travel bags on the second speeder. "Shall I run the preflight check while I wait?"

"Do that." Draxen nodded in agreement. "I can't wait to leave this failure behind. We've waisted a week here. It shouldn't take me more than a couple of hours." He started the engine, then took off in a cloud of dust.

Frustrated, Draxen accelerated until the engine

indicator on the speeder's display screen turned red —overheated.

Why in the stars did I listen to my parents' spirits and come to this savage world? There's nothing here.

With a tap on the screen, he switched to the map.

According to the coordinates now displayed, the forest, the last part of Ruesha he hadn't explored yet, was ahead, around one of the low, rounded mountains.

With a deep breath, he allowed the anger simmering under his skin to travel through him and to fill him with energy.

Not far from the small village where he'd spent the night, the waterfall offered a unique show with its purple color. The deep tint of the rock reflected through the curtain of falling water in all possible shades of violet, lavender, and mauves.

Beautiful, but still a waste of time. Draxen let out a sigh. *I have better things to do than wait for something to happen in this world. Like trying to find beautiful Master Charisse.*

Draxen veered the speeder around the curve of the mountain, and the waterfall disappeared from his view. According to his parents' spirits, he was supposed to witness a major event and reflect, as well as act upon, his actions to determine the future of the galaxy. *Not admire the scenery.* A new wave of anger prompted him to accelerate despite the narrow dirt road.

A disturbance in the surrounding energies tingled the base of his spine. Forced to slow at the edge of the forest, Draxen scanned the new landscape. Unfortunately, the massive tree trunks blocked the view. Alert, he let the energy guide him.

Hmm. Something doesn't feel right.

He continued on the black dirt road covered in places with thick patches of grass.

Maybe this is it? I'm supposed to do something that will influence future events in our galaxy, but what?

On reflex, he touched the weapon attached to his belt. The comfort brought by the black hilt washed over him like a cooling mist.

The more he advanced into the forest, the unsettled feeling of something being amiss became stronger. A sudden shift in the energies filled each muscle in his body with tension.

From the tumult in the energies swirling around, one presence hit him with familiarity.

Warm, calming, and invigorating, an avalanche of energy rolled over him. It felt the same way it did a little over two months ago, when he had first met the only woman he couldn't get out of his mind—Master Charisse Tarren.

Since the moment he saw her, Draxen had been taken by her outstanding beauty and radiating kindness. Antique paintings came to mind, illustrations of what some long-gone civilizations used to call *angels*. Silvery-white curls fell over her shoulders and past the waist line, framing a delicate face.

Her eyes, the color of melted chocolate, reflected genuine kindness and selflessness.

She's here, on this world. Her presence is unmistakable.

Just like a couple of months back, his heart gained speed, and the need to be close to her made him accelerate again. With each inch, he advanced deeper in to the forest. Danger thickened in the air.

At the grand celebration after the official peace treaty signing, Draxen tried to strike a conversation with her. Every one of his attempts had failed. The Master healer, whose reputation preceded her, brushed him off with cold and calculated politeness. She had straight-forward rejected him when he asked her to have coffee the next day.

Maybe because until not long ago, we'd been on the opposite sides of the war. The only plausible explanation he fabricated two months ago echoed, in his mind again. But she felt different from any other templars he'd ever met. There was a deep, well-hidden trace of darkness within her.

Templars were famous for the control they had over their emotions, keeping them locked away behind a solid wall. Master Charisse's barricade seemed to be cracked. She struggled to keep her emotions in check.

A parked speeder at the edge of the road yanked him back to reality and away from the web of his thoughts. Only steps away from it, a group of men clad in maroon-armored dress, held weapons pointed in a specific direction.

From behind one of the thick trees, their target came into view—Master Charisse Tarren. Draxen's heart flipped in his chest, hands tightened on the speeder's controls, and his foot slammed on the brake.

Why is she alone? Healers never travel by themselves.

His sudden stop and dismount off the speeder, attracted the attention of the attackers circling around her.

"Be on your way, Knight." One of the men directed his rifle toward him.

Tingles of energy coursed through his body, but Draxen continued his way to the woman who'd dominated his thoughts for the past couple of months.

"Master Charisse." He placed an open palm over his chest. "Who are these men? What do they want?"

"Lord Draxen." Her eyes widened with recognition and surprise. "They want to take me to their Master."

To be honest, she was the last person in the galaxy he expected to find in the world of Ruesha. Was this the event his parents had told him about? Would his next action change the fate of the galaxy? How? And what was he supposed to do?

Not leaving her with those guys, that's for sure.

"And who's that?" Draxen channeled his energy, drawing the power he needed to take down a dozen men with minimum damage not only to him, but to her as well.

"They wouldn't tell me." She kept her eyes trained on the attackers.

"Leave while you can, Knight." A threatening voice reached his ears through the drumming of his own pulse.

"It's Dark Lord." Draxen faced the man apparently in charge. "You'll do well to respect my hard-earned title." His hands closed into fists.

"Whatever." The same man waved a dismissive gloved hand. "Leave."

This is it—the moment I have to make my decision. He drew in a deep breath.

Draxen grabbed his weapon, activating it with one press of a button. The double-sized hilt expanded into a three-foot-long stave. Black metal poured from both ends, shaping into double-edged blades covered in bright-blue lighting.

He glanced over a shoulder at Charisse. Her protective shield seemed solid. Energy radiated from her like the sun between clouds after a torrential rain.

"Can you keep me alive, beautiful?" Draxen winked, hoping to defuse the tension coiled around her.

Instead of an answer, she nodded. Her hands danced in the air, forming a luminescent ball between opened palms.

"Stay behind me. This is going to be intense." He couldn't hold back a smile. "Short, but intense. It's time to see for myself all that healing you're famous for."

"Okay." Her cheeks covered in a pink dusting, matching her lips.

Draxen refocused on the men who changed targets, pointing their weapons toward him.

"Don't presume to tell me what to do." He took a few steps, placing himself between Charisse and the attackers. "Who's your Master?" Draxen tried to take a peek inside their minds. Protective barriers stopped him.

Hmm. Someone has them shielded.

"None of your business." The same man lifted a closed fist in the air, then dropped it, signaling to the others to open fire.

Warmth surrounded him. Minuscule glowing particles rained over him, invigorating each living cell in his body. A sheen of silver light coated him from head to toe, moments before the attackers opened fire.

She's powerful, indeed. This protective shield will be more than enough. Draxen whirled his weapon, lunging toward the enemy.

Screams mixed in the air with the whistle of the charges flying toward him. His blades reflected them back to the enemy. Each of his hits reached an intended target, cutting limbs and stabbing chests.

Dark, thick blood oozed from the wounds he had

caused, and fear rose from his attackers only to feed his power.

Like all Dark Knights, Draxen connected to the energies through his emotions—the more intensely he felt, the more power he gathered. But in combat, his kind also manipulated their adversaries' emotions, drawing extra power from them. It was the reason for which non-energy users didn't stand a chance in front of the Dark Knights.

The biggest challenge for him, and any other knight, was fighting templars and their lack of emotions.

One by one, the small army surrounding him and Charisse, fell to the ground, their blood soaking the lush grass.

Charisse's healing soothed the cuts caused by the grazing charges that sizzled against his skin. The protective shield she encased him in, absorbed most of the incoming damage.

She's brilliant. Hmm. What is that guy doing? Draxen rushed toward one of the men still standing, apparently sending a message from his bracer.

With one swift pass of his weapon, Draxen separated the man's arm from the rest of his body. On the second pass, the other end of the stave cut a diagonal line across his throat.

The display on the open bracer blinked like a warning: *Help*.

With only two of the attackers remaining, Draxen glanced toward Charisse. "This one sent an alarm. We'll have more company soon." He refocused, killing one more.

Draxen left the man in charge of the group for last. He jumped and twisted in the air, driving a foot to his opponent's chest. Knocked to the ground, and with his weapon out of reach, the defeated attacker didn't even attempt a recovery.

"Who is your Master?" Draxen placed his foot on the man's chest. "Why does he want her?"

For a second time, he tried to get inside the adversary's mind. The barrier protecting his thoughts stopped him.

"I will never tell you, Knight. You might as well kill me." Hatred coated his words. "Each of our deaths makes my Master stronger."

"Fanatic. As you wish." Draxen pushed a blade through the man's heart.

He took a moment to make sure all the attackers were dead, then retracted his weapon into the hilt and faced Charisse.

"Time to go. Nice healing, by the way." He

checked himself for any injuries. Other than a few cuts still healing, nothing but his robe had suffered serious damage. "I can see what everyone's raving about."

"Thank you." Charisse lowered her head with modesty. "Could you give me a ride? My speeder's dead."

"Sure." Draxen gestured toward his vehicle parked beside hers. "Where's your ship?" He headed to his ride.

"Ugh. . ." She followed him with hesitant steps. "On Rytherya."

"Then how did you get here, on Ruesha?" Draxen whirled on the heel of his boot to face her.

"With a public transporter." She clasped her hands together and avoided looking at him.

"Then, my ship it is." Draxen climbed on his speeder and started the engine. "Hop on." He patted the seat behind him.

Charisse grabbed a small backpack from her vehicle, then sat on the backseat.

"Sorry about all this. Thank you for your help." She placed the backpack's straps over her shoulders, then set her hands on his sides.

Draxen's heart slammed in his chest. In addition to the adrenaline still pumping through him, her close proximity sent his blood in a rush of flowing fire.

"My pleasure." He smiled, half turning toward her. "Hold on tight."

A timid smile parted her lips, and her arms tightened around him.

I can definitely get used to this.

3

Charisse

OF ALL THE *people in the galaxy, why did it have to be Him?* Charisse closed her eyes. *What is he doing on this world? Why is he here to start with?*

A sharp turn forced her to tighten her arms around Draxen before she went flying off the speeder.

His hard body, wrapped in black silk robes, delighted her fingertips. Currents, as subtle as an evening breeze, yet strong enough to send her heart racing, flowed from him through her being.

Without war and fighting, Charisse figured she could best help the people of the galaxy by ascending to the High Council. As soon as she solved the mystery of her identity, the celibacy oath would've been the next step. Only recently, a huge question mark lit-up over her decision.

Why does his proximity threaten the plans for the future? It should've been simple.

Ever since she first met Lord Draxen Harett, a couple of months ago, at the official peace treaty signing event, Charisse had a difficult time controlling her emotions around him. He definitely didn't fit her idea of a Dark Lord—a hate-filled soul.

His bluer than the sky eyes attracted her like a magnet despite any better judgement. Templars were taught to love all people, but discouraged to form attachments to any. Yet thin, invisible threads drew her toward the man she now hugged.

Roaring engines, coming from behind, made Charisse turn her head. More of the maroon-armored men, on speeders, approached in a cloud of dust.

"More of them now follow," She yelled in Draxen's ear, to make sure he heard her over the sound of the engines and the whistling air.

A crisp, woodsy scent wafted from him, soothing and inciting at the same time.

He glanced back with a frown. "Shield us and hold on."

Charisse nodded, shielding him. With her energy depleted, she didn't want to risk running out of defenses. There was no time to meditate and gather energy, so she had to rely on the slow, natural regeneration.

Bright red plasma charges resembling whistling arrows fired from behind. They sored through the air, zooming past them, except for one.

The hot streak of plasma grazed against her waist, above the left hip, forcing Charisse to bite her lips. Sharp pain coursed through her body, knocking the air out of her lungs.

Holding back a moan, she healed herself just enough to stop the bleeding, and refreshed the protective shield around Draxen.

Worried she won't have enough energy to take them through another possible fight, she preferred to endure the pain rather than fully heal herself.

The forest left behind served as a background every time she checked on the few speeders following them. The men chasing them kept a consistent distance. She leaned her head against Draxen's left shoulder blade.

He dialed a frequency on his bracer. The move-

ment made the muscles on his back tense and relaxe
a few times.

"Tosek, get ready to take off. Open the cargo
ramp and seal the main access." Draxen's voice rose
over all the noise around, vibrating in her ear. "Oh,
we'll have a guest aboard the ship, and we're coming
in hot." He terminated the connection.

"Who's Tosek?" She straightened with
curiosity.

"My assistant. Are you all right?" Draxen half
turned toward her. His gaze swept over the men
following them.

"I'm fine." Charisse forced a smile. "How much
longer?"

"We should be there in a few minutes, after we
make it around that waterfall up ahead." He accelerated, gesturing toward the right.

She stared at the breathtaking waterfall with its
streaks of sparkling violets mixed with lavender
ribbons in a hypnotic dance.

The *Waterfall of Dreams*, what locals had called
it, was supposed to fulfill a wish made from a pure
heart.

I wish to find out who I am, where my place is.
Eyes closed, Charisse sent her thoughts toward the
curtain of water. In response, subtle vibrations of

darkness radiated from the waterfall, as if possessed by a sleeping monster.

A new round of fire from behind yanked her back to reality.

This is stupid. Waterfalls don't turn wishes into reality. People do. She shook away the one moment of childish weakness and shielded Draxen again.

"We're almost there." Draxen's voice echoed in her ears.

One last turn on the winding road, and several ships parked in the open, came into view. Unlike most worlds, Ruesha didn't have much traffic, or a spaceport. A few designated places where ships could land, were scattered around the underpopulated world.

Of all the parked vessels, a slick silver one seemed ready for take-off, the grass around it flattened by the roaring engines.

As soon as the craft drove inside the cargo hold, Draxen hit the control panel, and the door slammed shut behind them. The next moment, the ship lifted off the ground.

"We're in." Draxen dismounted the speeder, turning toward her. "You're hurt." His gaze stopped on her injury.

Dried and fresh blood smudges marked her skin,

showing through the gap between the short, corseted blue top, and the waistband of the matching leather pants.

Arms around her, Draxen helped her off the speeder.

"I'll be fine. It's just a scratch." Charisse tried her best to hide the pain, but she favored her other leg.

Draxen's touch, the way his calloused hands felt on her body, made breathing almost impossible, as if all the oxygen had suddenly been vacuumed out of his ship. "I'll. . . ugh . . . heal m-myself when I recover some energy."

Doubt shadowed his eyes. "Here." He grabbed a healing patch from a pocket on his belt. "Use this until then." With gentle touches, he placed the patch over her wound.

Coolness spread from the small square infused with kovor, numbing her hip.

"Thank you." Charisse covered it with a hand.

"Can you walk?" He closed both his hands on her bare shoulders.

The touch sent her heart beating somewhere in her throat, and his sharp gaze, cutting through her like a laser, set the tips of her ears on fire.

"Of course." Charisse forced herself to take a few steps. "I can walk."

The ship tilted to the side, throwing her off balance and back into his arms.

For the love of stars, Tosek guy, fly straight.

"Doesn't look like it, beautiful." A smile parted his lips, revealing two symmetric dimples in his cheeks.

Charisse swallowed the lump in her throat, straightening. "Trust me, I'm fine." Grinding her teeth in pain, she started toward the stairs at one end of the cargo bay.

"You're stubborn." Draxen shook his head. "And definitely not fine." He helped her walk up the stairs and into the main area of his ship.

Each second in his close proximity, Charisse fought the impulse to lean against him. His body exuded power, and almost out of energy, she needed all of his support.

The circular center room, dominated by the middle holoprojector, welcomed her with an austere, clean décor.

Covered in black leather, a sofa followed the curve of the walls on one side. Built-in narrow partitions served as tables every two to three seats.

Charisse glanced over at the two droids, one on each side, plugged into recharging stations.

Hmm. The one to the left resembles my old TS2.

Draxen helped her sit. "Wait here." He crouched in front of her. "I'll check on Tosek, then be right back."

Charisse nodded. "Take your time." She made herself comfortable on the soft cushion. "I'll meditate and heal myself."

"All right." Draxen stood. He walked to the right, then over the threshold and on into the cockpit.

What in the stars is going on? I can't breathe when he's near me, yet miss him when he's away. She stared a few seconds at the doorway Draxen had used. *He's so different from any Dark Lord I have ever met. Why?*

Charisse took a deep breath, then closed her eyes. Arms in front of her, she focused, slipping into her meditative recovery state. Soothing calm enclosed her in a peaceful cocoon.

Draxen's image flickered to life in her mind. He'd probably expect some sort of an explanation, but he hadn't even flinched. The man simply trusted her, even risked his life and got her out of a tight situation.

Warmth spread inside her body at the memory of his touch.

Somehow, I doubt I'm ready for that celibacy oath.

ABOUT THE AUTHOR

Born and raised in Bucharest, Romania, Iuliana Foos currently lives with her husband in San Antonio, Texas.

When she doesn't daydream or write, she enjoys drinking copious amounts of coffee and playing online multiplayer games, hoping one day to have a white sanded beach as her backyard.

Becoming a traditionally published author has been a lifelong dream turned reality.

Made in the USA
Middletown, DE
12 October 2021